SURPRISE Lily

Surprise Lily

by
Sharelle Byars Moranville

HOLIDAY HOUSE · NEW YORK

Library of Congress Cataloging-in-Publication Data

Names: Moranville, Sharelle Byars, author.

Title: Surprise Lily / Sharelle Byars Moranville.

Description: New York : Holiday House, 2019. | Summary: "Happily living on
the family farm with just her grandmother, Rose's world is irrevocably
changed when her absent mother shows up out of the blue with a surprise
baby sister for Rose"—Provided by publisher.

Identifiers: LCCN 2019001264 | ISBN 9780823442645 (hardback)

Subjects: | CYAC: Family problems—Fiction. | Mothers and daughters—Fiction.
Toddlers—Fiction. | Grandmothers—Fiction. | Farm life—Fiction.
BISAC: JUVENILE FICTION/Family/Multigenerational.
JUVENILE FICTION/Lifestyles/Country Life. JUVENILE
FICTION/Social Issues/Adolescence.

Classification: LCC PZ7.M78825 Sur 2019 | DDC [Fic]—dc23

LC record available at https://lccn.loc.gov/2019001264

*L*ike the Lovells in this story, I grew up on a road where every farmhouse belonged to a Hawkins. While that hasn't been true for many years, my great-grandparents' home, the hub of this once all-family enclave, still houses the fifth generation. From my childhood, I remember waking up to the sound of coffee burbling through the percolator; I remember taking the first bite of biscuits and gravy every morning and watching the light shift in the sunroom as the day went by. I remember doing nothing much, yet having great adventures. I remember lying in the grass and staring up as swallows circled and dropped down the chimney one by one until the twilight sky was empty. I remember sleeping in the darkest of dark, in the quietest of quiet. Those are actually more than memories; they're important touchstones of my life. This story is dedicated to the beloved people of that time and place.

S.B.M.

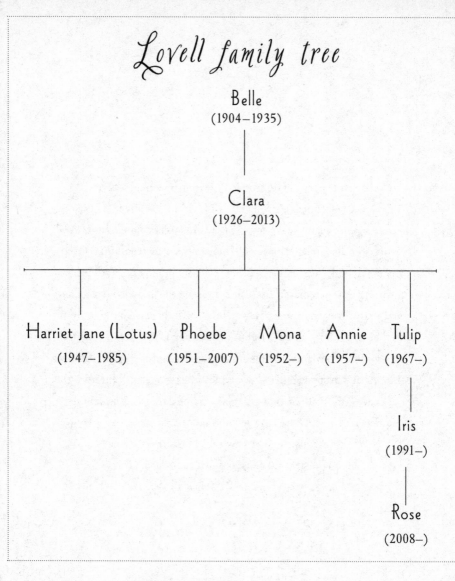

Lovell family tree

Belle
(1904–1935)

Clara
(1926–2013)

Harriet Jane (Lotus)   Phoebe   Mona   Annie   Tulip
(1947–1985)   (1951–2007)   (1952–)   (1957–)   (1967–)

Iris
(1991–)

Rose
(2008–)

Lovell family tree for Rose's fourth-grade oral report

one

Rose

ROSE threw on yesterday's clothes and hurried downstairs. She'd stayed awake worrying about her oral report and then had overslept.

In the mud room, she stepped into her boots, and ran along the lane to the barn. She waved at Ama—who the rest of the world called Tulip—as Ama was opening the chicken house door. Colorful birds flapped out, looking as groggy as Rose felt, and began their soft clucking.

Rose squinted against the morning light bouncing off the barn roof and the grain silo. Myrtle, their border collie, ran to greet Rose with a quick kiss on her wrist. Ama called, "How are you this morning?"

"I couldn't sleep," Rose said.

"Ah," Ama said, understanding. "You'll do fine today."

She might. But it was going to be so hard talking in front of everybody.

At the barn, Peanutbutter waited at the gate of her pen, dancing with eagerness. When Peanutbutter was born in March, her mama wouldn't claim her. So Ama and Rose had

1

carried the little calf to the barn and bottle-fed her and kept her warm and safe in a stall. She was a creamy tan color and had the softest eyes in the world, so they had named her Peanutbutter.

Grabbing the shears that hung outside Peanutbutter's stall, Rose said, "I'm hurrying as fast as I can."

Peanutbutter was old enough now that she had only an evening bottle. She ate fresh hay and dried calf food in the morning. There was an alfalfa pasture behind the barn and Rose cut a fistful of stems. She ran back to the pen and hand-fed Peanutbutter a few stems, then put the rest in the feeding tray.

Because she knew what was coming when Rose reached for the coil of rope, Peanutbutter ducked away. But Rose caught her and tied one end of the rope to the break halter and the other to a post. Cows were not by nature gentle to people, but in two months, Rose would need to lead Peanutbutter around at the fair as her 4-H project.

Peanutbutter yanked and tossed her head, but she'd learned that if she quit fighting, the break halter loosened, so she settled down and let Rose brush her and scratch under her chin. As she did every morning, Rose told her what a fine calf she was and how much she'd enjoy the fair.

Rose left Peanutbutter tied while she cleaned and refilled the water bucket, cleaned the food bucket, and weighed out dried food. Then she praised Peanutbutter for being a very good girl and untied her. Before she left, she fed Peanutbutter a handful of pellets, letting the calf suck her fingers.

"See you tonight," Rose said, wiping her hand on her shorts. "Wish me luck."

#

At the house, Rose washed her hands and face and brushed her teeth. Then, instead of changing into her usual clean shorts and T-shirt, she slid the hippie costume over her head. She draped the love beads she'd found in the attic around her neck. She put on her shoes, but this afternoon, before she stood and walked to the front of the room to give her oral report, she'd take them off so she'd look like her great-aunt in the photo.

Last night, Ama had dampened Rose's straight hair and braided it, and in bed Rose had tossed and turned with lumpy braids. Now she undid them and finger-combed her hair. She hoped her new style made her look kind of like Great-aunt Harriet Jane in the photograph—barefooted, wearing a flower child dress and love beads. Harriet Jane's long blond waves streamed in the wind, the Golden Gate Bridge in the background.

Rose zipped the photograph and family tree and note cards into her book bag. She swung the bag over her shoulder and ran downstairs.

In the kitchen, she poured a tiny bit of coffee into a cup and filled it with milk. She dropped two English muffin halves in the toaster and waited for them to pop up. The Westminster clock at the foot of the stairs chimed the quarter hour. They needed to leave soon.

The house was so quiet Rose could hear the ticks of the toaster heating. When the muffin was done, she buttered the halves on a paper towel and gulped her coffee, then went to meet Ama and Myrtle on their way back from the chicken house with a wire basket of eggs.

Before Ama took her half of the muffin, she slid her phone out of her jeans pocket. "Smile!" she said.

She snapped a picture of Rose, then turned the screen for Rose to see.

Rose took the phone and studied her image. She didn't look like herself. She looked older. She looked like her family—like the famous Lotus Lovell, aka Great-aunt Harriet Jane. And later she was going to stand in front of the whole class with naked feet and crazy hair. The kids would laugh. This was a terrible mistake. Like water going *glug, glug, glug* out of a bottle, her oral report went *glug, glug, glug* out of her head. Why hadn't she worn regular clothes and regular hair?

"What's wrong?" Ama said.

"I forgot my report," Rose said in a small voice, giving back Ama's phone.

Ama hugged her shoulders. "Everything will be fine. You'll see."

Rose, her appetite gone, tossed the rest of her English muffin to Myrtle.

"What are you doing today?" she asked Ama as they got in the car.

Ama's face lit up. "Can you believe cutting hay? The weather gods are smiling. We haven't made hay this early for a long time. Hopefully, we can get a second cutting off that ground this year. Which means more to sell this winter."

"Don't forget to leave a patch for Peanutbutter."

"I won't."

They rode in silence after that, Ama probably planning the details of her day as Rose took her note cards out of her backpack, her hands trembling. She hated the way her hands shook when she was nervous. She'd felt so confident last night. She'd memorized exactly what she was going to say until it was perfect. The note cards were just for show and because the teacher said she had to have them. She didn't need them. Or she hadn't needed them. But now, even when she looked at the cards, the flow of words wouldn't come back.

She put the cards away and studied the family tree she and Ama had made.

Great-great-grandmother Belle had been beautiful and died tragically young, leaving her heartbroken little girl behind. The angel in the cemetery, standing taller than the other markers, was in Belle's honor. The fancy bed Belle bought for her daughter, Clara, had been passed down through the Lovell girls and Rose still slept in it.

Clara had grown up to have five daughters and cherished them like rubies. Of those five, Harriet Jane had run off to San Francisco and become Lotus Lovell, the famous hippie artist who had died young from cancer. Phoebe and Mona, almost like twins, had grown up and lived happily ever after until Aunt Phoebe died before Rose was born. Aunt Phoebe had been Uncle Thomas's mother. Aunt Mona had children and grandchildren too and most of that family lived in Florida. Annie, who, according to Ama, had been the best big sister in the world, was now a pediatrician living in Portland, Oregon. Tulip had become Ama—the polestar in Rose's sky. And Ama and Rose farmed the land Lovells had owned in Southern Illinois for over a hundred years.

Rose had thought about leaving Iris, her mother, off the family tree because Rose wasn't going to talk about her in the report. She was mainly going to talk about Harriet Jane aka Lotus. But a family tree should be accurate, so she and Ama had included Iris. Plus, if she hadn't, some kid might have pointed it out. Everybody at school knew she had a mother. Some of the kids' parents had even known Iris in high school. And now and then, people said mean things like how her mother was a druggie who'd abandoned Rose when Rose was a baby. But Rose ignored them because she truly didn't care. She had everything she needed or wanted. Ama and Myrtle. A big farmhouse full of family and history. Bottle calves. Cows, ponds, pastures, and woods. The sun, the moon, the stars. Her kingdom reached as far as her eyes could see and as high as the sky could reach.

Lovell family tree

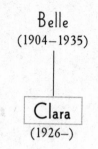

Belle
(1904–1935)

Clara
(1926–)

·· two ··

Clara
1936

$\mathcal{A}$WAKENED by birdsong, Clara sat up and looked out the window. The big cloudless sky was turning pink.

Beyond the well and beyond the garden, the door of the outhouse opened and her daddy stepped out. Tall and big-shouldered, he came toward the house in his bib overalls. His first name, Franklin, was the same as President Roosevelt's, which Clara thought fitting. He could be president of the United States if he had time. The garden gate squeaked as he opened it.

Clara had planted many of the things growing in the garden. She'd scattered carrot seeds, as fine as sugar, hoping the wind didn't carry them off before she got them covered. She'd poked puckered-up pea seeds into the dirt an inch deep, every two inches. It had been hard to stay straight. Her daddy said the pea patch looked like ruffles instead of rows. She didn't understand why straightness was so valued.

She went out in her nightgown barefooted. Each morning, they watered the garden while the plants were still fresh from the night air.

Her daddy had let out the chickens and they clucked and pecked for bugs in the grass.

At the well, she pumped water, sending it gushing into a pail and splashing on her feet. The droplets rolled off onto the concrete curb. Curling her toes, she clung to the cool wetness.

When two buckets were full, her daddy came and got them. "How are you this morning?" he asked.

"Fine," she said, following with long-handled dippers.

Should she mention what day this was, or should they pretend it was any old day?

If her mother hadn't died last November, she would have been thirty-two today, and they would have turned themselves inside out trying to make her happy. Clara had tried to honor her mother like the Commandments said, but her mother had shown in a hundred ways she hadn't *felt* honored, so Clara's efforts had been a fizzle.

Her mama had pined away. That was what everybody in the family said. *Poor Belle just pined away.* It made Clara burn with shame because it meant they weren't good enough to live for. There were a million preferable things her mother could have died from. Childbirth, consumption, lockjaw, rabies, appendicitis, drowning, a broken neck. Or she could have let them make her happy so she didn't pine away. And if she'd let them make her happy and died of something normal, Clara would have been heartbroken. Then she would have been normal too.

But she was an awful sinner because deep down she liked life better without her mother.

Clara and her daddy normally talked while they worked. About things they'd done yesterday or were going to do today. But this morning they were quiet.

Finally, her daddy said, "Just think about how happy she is in heaven now."

The heaven Clara heard about at church was nothing but a higher, shinier version of this life where you saw the same old people all the time. Her mother would pine away there too.

"You know what I think?" she asked.

He shook his head.

"Well, you know how Mama has those postcards from her friend Josephine—the one who travels and lives in foreign countries. And you know how Mama mooned over those pictures of the Leaning Tower of Pisa and all those statues of naked people. And how she never stopped going on about what a good time Josephine was having."

"Sure. Your mama wanted to travel. She didn't bargain on hard times and being stuck out here with nothing to do."

"Well, I think Mama's traveling. I think she's living in an apartment in Rome above one of those cafés. And she and Josephine drink coffee and take long walks and talk to interesting people. I'll bet Mama can even speak Italian now. That could be part of the mystery and miracle of what happens when a person dies. They can speak any language without having to learn it. I'll bet she can speak Latin if she wants to."

Her dad groped for the bandana in his pocket and pretended to wipe away sweat. Clara went and leaned against his side.

She waited, smelling the nose-twitching scent of wet earth where they'd poured water around the plants. She watched the sky. Rain would make everything better.

Her daddy took away the bandana and looked down at her, his eyes red. "That's a fine way to think of things, Clara. You're a good girl."

No, she was not. She was just trying to make herself feel better for being a bad person.

"I'm glad we were able to put that angel in the cemetery for her," he said.

She gazed into the distance as if contemplating how beautiful the angel was, when in fact she hated the thing. Everybody else's marker was no higher than a yardstick, so the angel just made people talk more. *Poor tragic Belle. Pined away.*

The bottle calf bawled, saying *Don't forget me!* The sun was all the way up and the heat was beginning. Her daddy stretched his back. Watering the garden was harder for him because he was so tall.

When they finished, they did rock-paper-scissors to see who got to feed the calf. Her daddy won.

"I'll make breakfast," she said.

They walked toward the house, leaving the pails and dippers

at the well. While they were there, her daddy dropped a bucket down on a rope and drew up a pail of water. Pump water tasted like metal. This water tasted so good it was hard to stop gulping. A puff of breeze blew her nightgown away from her sweaty body.

As her daddy went to feed the calf, Clara washed her face and hands in the enamel basin at the kitchen window. She tried to scrub away the smell of the pump handle. Then she set the basin on the floor and stood in it. She wiggled her toes and rubbed one wet foot on top of the other, wishing she could stand there all day. But finally, she stepped out and dried her feet.

In the yard, she dumped the basin on the lilac bush. The blossoms were scrawny, but they smelled good. She found the scissors and snipped a few and put them in a pale blue Mason jar. They were very pretty in that jar. She liked the way the water seemed to bend the twiggy stems. That was called refraction. She was just finishing fourth grade, but because all fifteen kids were in one room at school, she got to hear what the eighth graders were learning.

She left the lilacs on the counter for her daddy to see. He might want to take them to her mama's grave.

She was finishing frying the bacon her daddy had brought in from the smokehouse yesterday when he came to wash up. She fried eggs and sliced bread off the loaf one of the aunts had sent over with one of the cousins yesterday. She smeared a little jelly on each slice and filled their plates.

They ate in the porch swing, looking at the pasture and the

woods beyond. Before they took their plates out, she had put water on the stove to heat.

The porch was on the west side where it was cool in the morning. Her legs didn't reach the porch floor, but her daddy rocked them back and forth.

"After I do chores, we're going over to Dad's to get the new corn planter ready," he said. "Everybody will be there. That'll take our minds off what day this is."

President Roosevelt said on the radio times were getting better, and that was why all the Lovells had pitched in to buy the corn planter that would plant four rows at a time. She just hoped rain came to water in the corn. She could see them out there with buckets and dippers, the whole Lovell clan, taking care of everybody's fields. She giggled.

"What's funny?"

She told him.

He smiled and bumped her with his arm. "Don't worry, sugar. It will rain. It always does."

While her dad was milking their Jersey cow and slopping the hogs, Clara put their dishes to soak in the warm water from the stove; then she went to make her bed. She still slept in the baby room, although she was ten. How many times had she heard her mother say *She's still in the baby room, Franklin. It's not right.* There was a big upstairs for bedrooms, but it didn't have floors or ceilings or walls yet. It had been part of her daddy's plan to build a fine house for his fine bride where they would raise a fine family.

But the times had changed and they'd been lucky to hang on to their land and tractor. And they had the necessary things—a well, a garden, an outhouse, a smokehouse, a chicken house, a hog house, a barn, and a corncrib.

The big house had been a great beginning, just like her mama's clock with Westminster chimes people made such a fuss over. And her mama's fine wardrobe with its red enamel drawers. And Clara's own fancy bed.

The bed was a white concoction (a vocabulary word from the sixth graders) that made her think of a birdcage. Or maybe a wedding cake because it was so high. She'd needed a step stool to get in it when she was small. Now she could do a little jump. The headboard and footboard were made of curling metal vines. Birds, their beaks open, sang silently. Nobody in the countryside had such a fine bed.

For a minute, she watched her daddy coming down the lane from the barn. He grabbed the bucket that hung on a nail by the henhouse door and went inside. She was glad he was going to gather the eggs because she didn't like to. The chicken house was hot and dusty and sometimes the hens pecked her hand when she reached for the eggs.

She stripped off her gown and hung it on a peg, took her dress off the other peg, and slipped it over her head. She put on clean underpants, then sat on her hope chest—the only other piece of furniture in the room—to put on her socks and shoes. Grandpa Lovell made cedar hope chests for the girl cousins on their tenth birthdays. By the time they were married, hopefully the chests would be full of useful things like tea towels and dishes and pretty nightgowns.

Clara loved the plain cedar chest that smelled so good, but she didn't invest much energy in hoping someday somebody might want to marry her. She hoped it would rain. She hoped the garden would grow. She hoped her mama was happy in Italian heaven. She hoped her daddy stayed strong and well. She hoped she was a good daughter and would become a better person. She hoped the uncles would make ice cream today. She hoped until she had touched on all the important stuff. And then she said *Amen*.

#

As they walked to Grandma and Grandpa Lovell's, her daddy looked at the pasture beside the road and said it was about played out. "We'll move those cows tomorrow," he said.

She liked moving cows. They were gentle and followed her daddy, who carried a bucket of grain and called *suk suk*. She brought up the rear, clapping at the laggards. She liked the cows more than she liked the chickens or the hogs.

At the cemetery at the end of the road, she wondered if they would go inside to visit her mother's grave. She'd forgotten about the Mason jar of flowers. But her daddy looked at the angel from the road and then they turned east.

Uncle Robert and Aunt Marie's house was at the top of the hill. It was a yellow two-storied among the trees with a barn and shed behind it. Her cousins' rope swing hung from a giant oak tree in the side yard. They flew so high in that swing Clara felt like her toes almost touched heaven.

"They must already be gone," her daddy said.

Their little mare nickered and trotted to the fence. Clara jumped the ditch and petted her.

At the bottom of the hill, an almost-dry creek, choked with grass, ran under a wooden bridge. The sound was hollow beneath her daddy's boots.

On top of the next hill was Uncle Samuel and Aunt Ruth's place. Aunt Ruth was shaking a rug on the front porch. She waved and called, "The kids are just picking a mess of asparagus for the meal. Be there in two shakes of a lamb's tail."

Aunt Ruth talked funny because she was from Tennessee.

"See you there," her daddy called, glancing at Clara with a hidden smile.

At the bottom of the hill, they stopped on the bridge to see if there was any water flowing. There wasn't, but her daddy spotted a box turtle in the grass.

"It looks like his shell is painted with hieroglyphs," she said.

He looked at her.

"Seventh graders," she explained. "Ancient Egyptian writing."

The next hill belonged to Uncle Joseph and Aunt Treva. Their new puppy yapped ferociously from the wraparound porch.

"He thinks he's the king of the hill," her daddy said, laughing.

"I would like to have a puppy."

She got to play with her cousins' puppies. But she wanted one that she could be the boss of. One that might like to sleep in her room.

Her mama had always said no. One dog meant more dogs and nonsense she didn't want to deal with.

Her daddy didn't say anything but he squeezed her shoulder in a promising way.

The road bent north. In the fencerows, wild morning glory climbed over everything. Hidden birds tweeted and mystery critters rustled around.

Soon they came to Miss Doll's house. Miss Doll was the widowed mother of Aunt Ruth. Her house was so tiny they called it the dollhouse. It was surrounded by an ornate black metal fence with spikes that fired Clara's imagination. When she squinted her eyes and stared at the bark of the old hickory trees that surrounded the house, she saw hideous faces that shifted their expressions more the longer she looked. But the faces disappeared when she tried to get her cousins to see them.

The road bent east and they crossed the railroad track on a bridge high above it. Then around the next bend was Grandma and Grandpa Lovell's gingerbread house with the pump organ in the parlor and the big barn with the sparkling pond behind it.

She saw cousins fishing from the bank. She glanced at her daddy, who looked happier than he'd looked all morning.

"You go ahead, sugar." He touched her head. "Have a good time with your cousins."

It seemed wicked on this day.

"Go on," he said. "Catch us a fish."

She took off running. Being set free to have fun was almost as good as rain.

Lovell family tree

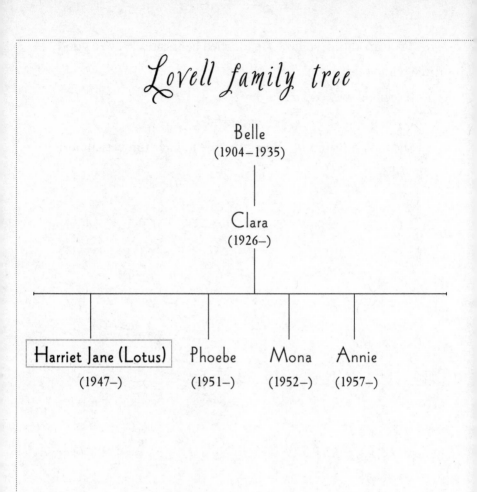

Belle
(1904–1935)

Clara
(1926–)

Harriet Jane (Lotus)
(1947–)

Phoebe
(1951–)

Mona
(1952–)

Annie
(1957–)

··three··

Harriet Jane
1957

WHEN her dad came in from the field for lunch, Harriet Jane was at the counter stirring sugar into the iced tea. She looked away when he kissed her mom on the lips.

He ruffled Harriet Jane's bangs as he walked past. "How's my number one daughter?"

"Fine," she said.

He picked up baby Annie and nuzzled her. Then he made a face and put her back in her playpen. "Clara, the baby needs her diaper changed," he said.

Her mother looked up from the potatoes she was whipping. Her eyes went to Harriet Jane, then to the baby, and back to Harriet Jane.

Harriet Jane's dad had gone into the dining room and sat down in his chair at the head of the table and opened the day-old newspaper the mail carrier had just delivered. Harriet Jane had run out to the mailbox to get it because she knew her dad would like to look at it.

"Call Phoebe and Mona," their mother told Harriet Jane.

"Tell them it's time to eat. And please change Annie. I'm in the middle of getting food on."

Harriet Jane went to the bottom of the stairs and was starting to yell up when the Westminster clock started its noonday extravaganza. Sixteen chimes—four for the quarter hour, four more for the half hour, four more for the three-quarters hour, four more for the full hour—followed by twelve slow, hearty bongs. While she waited for it to end, she congratulated herself on having used her word for the day in a sentence. *Extravaganza.* It meant an elaborate or spectacular entertainment or production. An aunt had given her a Word a Day calendar for Christmas.

When the old clock finally stopped vibrating, she yelled, "Phoebe! Mona! Come on! Time to eat!"

She heard the scramble of their shoes on the wood floors overhead as she picked up Annie and carried her to the baby bedroom.

The downy softness of her sister's almost-bald head brushed against her cheek. "You're a bald, smelly baby," she whispered in Annie's ear.

Annie beamed and Harriet Jane kissed her, her heart overflowing despite the messy little bottom she was about to clean.

In the baby bedroom, she laid Annie on the changing table. Annie gazed up at her big sister as if Harriet Jane were the most wonderful thing on the planet. Why did the spirit from the place where all the plants were dead and the creeks were full of sludge and the sun never shone come to sit on her then? Force tears to her eyes? Make her ache deeper than her bones?

She tried to keep what happened secret. If she was a good big sister, got perfect grades, helped her mother, learned a word a day, and won blue ribbons, she would make everybody proud—Grandpa Lovell, her parents, her teachers, her 4-H leader. Her dad. Then the spirit would leave her alone and nobody would ever know.

She forced herself to make a silly noise and bury her face in Annie's fat little neck, giving big smooches, making her baby sister crow with laughter.

"We're waiting," their dad called from the dining room. "Food's getting cold."

After she'd put Annie in the high chair and sat down, their dad said grace. He always began by thanking God for each one of them by name, starting with her mother. Harriet Jane felt a glow every time when her daddy thanked God for her. Then he asked for forgiveness of their sins, known and unknown. Then he asked God to please hold off the rain until all the corn was in the ground because if he couldn't finish in the next couple of days, it would be too late for the year.

Harriet Jane knew he'd worried about the cold, wet spring that had kept farmers out of the field. Every morning and every evening he'd hung on the weather report, longing for warm, dry days.

After the critical stuff—gratitude, forgiveness, weather—he talked to God about whatever was on his mind. Sometimes it didn't take long. Other times the food got cold. Today, Annie smacked the high chair tray, and Harriet Jane sensed their mother's hands going over Annie's as her dad discussed the neighbor who had bought Uncle Joseph's house and was letting the place get junky. When her dad finally said *Amen*, he looked at Harriet Jane. "I thought you were going to town with the 4-H kids. Weren't you guys going to the swimming pool this afternoon?"

"I didn't want to," she said.

"Why not?" he asked. "I thought you did."

She shrugged. "I changed my mind."

It felt like too much trouble. And her swimsuit didn't fit.

Her dad looked perplexed. Another one of her Word a Day achievements. It meant baffled or puzzled. "Did you know about this, Clara?" he asked their mother, who had food in her mouth but nodded.

But Harriet Jane was pretty sure her mother had forgotten the swimsuit was too short and tight, and Harriet Jane hadn't reminded her a second time that she needed a new one. It was hopeless anyway. The new swimsuit would be either too babyish or too sophisticated.

Phoebe and Mona started teasing each other and Mona finally got mad and kicked Phoebe. The baby dropped her spoon on the floor and began to fuss for someone to pick it up. The phone rang and Harriet Jane's mother got up to answer it and everybody forgot about Harriet Jane not going swimming.

#

It was hot upstairs, but the windows were open and a breeze tickled her neck. The whir of the Singer came from the sewing room downstairs, where their mother was making Phoebe and Mona look-alike dresses. Their mother sewed all their clothes except their underwear. Everybody said the girls always looked so pretty, and Clara so fashionable.

Except for the sound of the sewing machine, it was quiet. The baby was napping. Phoebe and Mona were in Mona's room being completely still, which meant they had fallen asleep, which they often did on warm afternoons, or they were doing something they shouldn't, like giving each other haircuts or playing with their mother's lipstick.

She should hear the sound of the tractor. Maybe her dad had shut down to refill the planter. She listened, hoping the tractor would start again so she didn't have to worry.

He was so proud of her. She wished she could tell him about the gray spirit and how tired it made her. She thought he could do something about the spirit if he knew. There was no reason for her to be tired. She didn't have too much work to do. Her mother wanted her to have fun, be happy, read, draw, pursue her dreams, go swimming. Sometimes she could do those things, and sometimes she couldn't. If she told her dad, he'd know there was something wrong with her and wouldn't be proud of her anymore.

When the tractor started up again, she felt giddy with relief. She sank to the floor cross-legged in front of the beautiful old wardrobe at the end of the hall.

The wardrobe had belonged to their grandmother Belle Lovell, who had died a long time ago. Eventually, Grandpa Lovell took a second wife, and when their mother married their daddy, Ralph Hoffmann, Grandpa Lovell moved with his second wife to town, where he ran a grain elevator with his new wife's cousin. Grandpa Lovell gave the house and the farm to his beloved Clara and her new husband.

Their daddy had made changes after he got home from the army. He tore down the dim, dusty corncrib where cracks of sunlight shone between the boards, and he installed a shiny new grain bin. He got rid of the chicken house and the hog pen because he wanted to concentrate on cattle and grain farming. When they got running water in the house and a real bathroom, they didn't need the outhouse anymore. He wanted to knock down the smokehouse, but their mama convinced him to leave it for a garden shed. Inside the house, all of Grandma Belle's fine things, like the wardrobe, the Westminster grandfather clock, and the bed Harriet Jane slept in, stayed.

The wardrobe loomed at the end of the hall, seeming to hint at answers to questions Harriet Jane didn't have yet. There were things in the drawers her parents wouldn't think were suitable for her to be looking at. She especially loved the postcards—both the pictures on the front and what was on the back. She had looked at them many times when her mother thought she was in her room reading. She had grouped them by sender. The ones from Josephine were the best because they had foreign language on the back that explained what was on the front. Harriet Jane liked to flip them back and forth, trying to figure out from the picture what the Italian words might say.

Many of Josephine's postcards showed enormous naked statues, lots of them in fountains. Harriet Jane had never seen a naked man and she studied those pictures. There were naked ladies too. And kids and babies. Even the animals looked naked as spouts of water jetted up among the figures or poured out of the mouths of fish.

"Harriet Jane?" her mother called.

She closed the drawer and jumped up, going to the top of the stairs.

"I have an idea," her mother said. "Come down and let's talk about it."

In the sewing room, the pretty sundresses were spread out on the cutting table. Harriet Jane hoped her mother's idea wasn't to also make her one. Phoebe and Mona were cute little girls. Harriet Jane would look like a giraffe in a tutu. At school, kids called her Giraffe. And Stretch. Maybe people expected so much of her because she was tall.

"Why don't I make you a swimsuit?" her mother asked.

Harriet Jane thought swimsuits, like underwear, had to come from the store or the Sears catalogue.

Her mother opened her cedar hope chest, which sat under the south window. She held up two pieces of fabric. One was white with little black dots. One was black with big white dots. "What do you think?" she asked.

Harriet Jane was glad her mother hadn't picked something babyish like the gingham she'd used for the little girls' sundresses.

"Maybe," she said. A swimsuit made out of the polka dots could be cute.

"Slip off your clothes and let me measure you."

The soft tape measure felt cool against her skin as her mother measured around her chest under her arms. Then she measured the distance between the two bumps on Harriet Jane's collarbone. Her soft hands with their light touch smelled like soap and cigarettes. Harriet Jane remembered that scent from way back when there had been only her, and her mother had brushed her hair every morning and put in barrettes.

Her mother made notes, then measured the length of Harriet Jane's body from a point on her chest to her crotch. She wrote down that number. Then she did the same thing on Harriet Jane's back.

Harriet Jane could see herself in the standing mirror. Naked except for her panties, her frizzy blond hair pulled back in a ponytail, she was gawky and ugly.

Her mother caught her eyes in the mirror. "You probably don't realize it, honey," she said, "but you're starting to look so much like your grandmother Lovell."

Harriet Jane stared at the image in the mirror. Why did her mother say that? Grandmother Lovell—Belle—had been beautiful. Everybody said so. And there were pictures in the wardrobe. Harriet Jane had seen with her own eyes how pretty she was.

"Really?" she asked, wanting to believe.

"Really," her mother said.

"What did she die of, Mama?"

Her mother was busy writing. Finally, she looked up. "Back then, people died of all kinds of things. It's not like now where we hop in the car and go to the doctor and get a penicillin shot when we get sick or hurt. Back then, people just died more."

How terrible. Thank goodness they lived now instead of then so their mother wouldn't die of any of those things. She couldn't leave them because she filled up all the space between and around them clear to the sky. Sometimes she sat on the couch and invited her four children to pile on, and she kissed the tumble of them—faces, elbows, hands, heads, even feet— asking them if they were happy. Everybody but the baby said *Yes, Mama*. When she had to lie, Harriet Jane felt guilty.

She put her arms around her mother, who kissed her on the head and held her close. Harriet Jane was getting so tall it felt strange to be cuddled.

Finally, her mother gave her a squeeze and stepped away. "I'm going to the garden for a while. I need to stretch. Will you listen for the kids? If the baby wakes up, bring her out to me."

Harriet Jane nodded.

Her mother tied her hair with a scarf and put on sunglasses.

When she was on her way to the garden, Harriet Jane went into the baby bedroom very quietly so she didn't wake Annie, who slept on her back, her arms out, her face turned to the side, a little dark spot of drool on the crib sheet.

They had all slept in the baby bedroom until, like birds leaving the nest, they flew upstairs and landed in their real bedrooms.

Through the window, she could see her mother working in the garden. Their mother didn't can and freeze and pickle and preserve like their relatives along Lovell Road did. She said anything that had to be canned or frozen, she'd buy at Kroger's, thank you. But she did like to grow food they'd eat fresh. Peas that were sweet as candy, which Harriet Jane liked to eat right off the plant, standing in the garden with the sun on her shoulders. Fat watermelons that weighed a ton and dripped off your chin onto your arms and the tops of your feet.

There was an old pump that squealed like a pig when anybody moved the handle, but it was a good place to wash dirty feet and hands. The water was always cold.

Harriet Jane thought of the swimming pool. How good the water would feel rising up around her shoulders. How long she'd stay cool afterward. She thought of the icy sweetness of the snow cones from the concession stand and how they stained her mouth. It probably would have been fun to go. She would go next time.

She went upstairs and peeked in on the girls in Mona's room.

They were sound asleep. She glanced into Phoebe's empty room, where a giant pink panda sat in the corner. There was a room waiting for Annie, right across the hall from Harriet Jane. Maybe their mother would have more babies and they'd have to share bedrooms. Phoebe and Mona could share. They almost did anyway.

She went into her own room. The cousins and her friends teased her about her bed because it was so old-fashioned, but she loved it. It made her think of a pretty cage that didn't keep her in but let her keep the rest of the world out when she needed to. But she didn't need to now. The spirit from the bad place was lifting. She felt better. Like nothing bad could ever happen to any of them. Like she could do anything.

She got her crayons and colored pencils and inks and brushes and went to the north wall, where there were no doors or windows to break up the smooth surface. Her cousins were openmouthed that she was allowed to do this. The first time, about six months ago, she hadn't had permission. She'd just done it. She'd been looking at Josephine's postcards and admiring the way artists painted on the walls and ceilings. She stood up feeling so strong. She could do that too. Her room would be as beautiful as the Sistine Chapel.

With joy surging through her, she'd drawn big things with her crayons and chalk. Trees and flowers and people and houses and hills and clouds as high as she could reach standing on her desk. She'd forgotten time and where she was. Then she'd gradually fallen back to earth and known she was in terrible trouble. *Why* had she done such a thing?

Her mother hadn't discovered the ruined wall for two days. During that time, dread trailed Harriet Jane.

One afternoon her mother brought in Harriett Jane's freshly ironed clothes, smelling like spray starch, to hang in the closet.

She stopped. She stared, frozen.

Harriet Jane was on her bed reading *Blue Willow*. She wanted to vanish. She waited for her mother to yell. To say she couldn't believe Harriet Jane had done such a thing. To tell her to stay in her room until her daddy got in from the field. Harriet Jane almost threw up at the idea of his knowing. She had never done such a disobedient thing. She might get a spanking. It wouldn't hurt much, but it would break her heart. And her daddy's heart.

She waited, wishing her mother would go ahead and yell.

Finally, her mother sat on the bed, her eyes still on the ruined wall.

"That looks so joyful," she said. She was crying.

Harriet Jane stared in horror. Her mother never *ever* cried. "I'm sorry," she said, starting to cry herself. "I'm sorry, Mama."

Her mother turned her face away, but she caught Harriet Jane's hand. Finally, she took a deep breath and let it out. She wiped her face with her hands. "A long time ago I knew someone like you. Someone who often felt really sad."

Harriet Jane stared. How did her mother know?

Her mother made a humming sound and stared at the wall. "I think your art is beautiful," she said. Her face looked strange and broken like she needed to cry and smile at the same time. "Just beautiful." She brushed away tears. "Go ahead and do it when you feel like it. I'll talk to your dad."

Her dad never said anything about this strange indulgence. Harriet Jane kept expecting he might talk to God about it during grace, but thank goodness he didn't. There was puzzlement in the back of his eyes sometimes when he looked at her, and she was afraid she'd disappointed him.

When the dark spirit dragged her down, it helped to go to the walls of her room and fight back. She wondered who her mother had known long ago who often felt really sad.

Lovell family tree

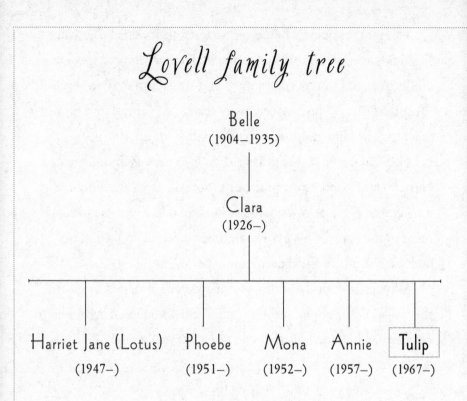

Belle
(1904–1935)

Clara
(1926–)

Harriet Jane (Lotus)
(1947–)

Phoebe
(1951–)

Mona
(1952–)

Annie
(1957–)

Tulip
(1967–)

··four··

Tulip
1977

$\mathcal{T}$ULIP woke up and instantly knew what was different and special about the house. Her sister Annie was asleep in the bedroom across the hall. Annie had a red car, three boyfriends, and plans to spend a lot of time with Tulip this summer. Or so Tulip hoped.

The smell of coffee and the drone of the TV drifted upstairs as she peeked into the jumble of Annie's room across the hall. The sun bathed it in light, picking out the details of Annie's suitcases and laundry bags and boxes of books from her dorm room. Annie's strawberry-blond hair shone like real gold in the sun. Annie made Tulip think of a peach, and Tulip loved peaches. She loved Annie. She loved her other sisters too, of course, but they were much older. More like aunts. Annie was only twenty. Twice as old as Tulip, but not *that* old.

Annie's white peasant blouse was tossed on the floor. Tulip crept into the room and picked it up because Annie was kind of a slob. Before Tulip laid it on a chair, she held it to her face. When she was little and her feet were cold, Annie let Tulip get in bed with her until they were toasty, and then Annie piggybacked Tulip back to her own bed. Tulip loved the way Annie's pillows smelled. When Annie first went to college, Tulip got into her bed one night. But it made her so lonesome she never did it again.

She listened for the sound of the new tractor and thought she heard it far in the distance where her dad was working on the acreage he'd bought from Aunt Marie after Uncle Robert died last year. Tulip's mother said her dad was spending money like there was no tomorrow. He patted her on the behind and said there would always be a tomorrow.

Tulip would probably be on the tractor with him this morning if it weren't Annie's first day home. Tulip went to the bull sales with him and watched the beautiful animals in the arena and told her dad the ones she would buy if she had money.

Downstairs, she poured a glass of orange juice. She saw her mother out in the garden, the ties of her sun hat ruffling in the breeze.

On her way to the garden, Tulip snapped off a lilac blossom and held it to her nose.

Her mother was on her knees harvesting spinach and lettuce. "How's my little Tulip?" she asked, standing up.

Tulip used to love having a fancy name, especially when her sisters had such ordinary ones. But now *Tulip* was starting to feel babyish. Especially when it was *my little Tulip*. Plus, her cousin Thomas—who was really her nephew, but almost her same age—had a collie pup he named Marigold, which she thought he did on purpose to annoy her.

"Why did you name me that?"

"Don't you like the name?" her mother asked.

"Kind of. I guess. But everybody else has a normal one."

Her mother brushed Tulip's hair off her face and behind her ear. "You were a surprise so you got a special name."

Tulip held the lilac blossom out to her mother, who brushed it beneath her nose, then tucked it into her hatband.

"Mom, if we cut that old bush way back, it would bloom better next year."

Her mother smiled. "The things you know."

Tulip shrugged. She noticed and remembered things having to do with plants and animals. She was going to grow up and farm forever. People said *You mean you're going to marry a farmer.* That was not what she meant.

"Is Annie still sleeping?" her mom asked.

"Yes. Do you think I should wake her?"

"Not yet," her mom said. "But when she gets up I want you two to go into town and get flowers for the cemetery. Then weed and trim around the graves, scrub the bird poop off the markers, and make them look nice like you always do. Memorial Day is around the corner."

Good. She was going to spend the day doing something with Annie. Even if Annie decided she'd rather be with friends, their mother *said*.

But Annie didn't complain when she finally woke up after Tulip made as much noise as it was possible to make and still have it seem accidental.

"Okay, okay," Annie called.

A while later, Tulip sat on the edge of the bathtub watching Annie blow out her long hair and make it really big. She wore a pair of cutoffs and a white T-shirt, and at the last minute she added a pale blue bandana, rolled and tied around her neck. It made her blue eyes glow and her freckles stand out. She looked so beautiful Tulip could hardly stand it. Then she put on a pair of wedge sandals and stood three inches taller.

Tulip flung her arms around her sister. "Let's go!"

They loaded the trunk of Annie's car with a broom, four plastic jugs of water, a bucket, rags, and clippers.

As they left, Tulip saw her dad with the builders who were putting up the fancy new pole barn. It would be one long building with a barn, a machine shed, and a shop for welding and machinery repair all in one.

"You want to see what Dad's doing?" she asked Annie.

"Why don't you tell me?" Annie said.

And so Tulip did, ending with, "The shop will have a concrete floor. And a bathroom! And there will be a refrigerator for storing medicine for the cattle and a hot plate for heating calf formula."

Annie laughed. "How about a TV?"

Tulip said no, then realized Annie was teasing.

"And when the barn is finished, we're going to build a bunker silo."

She waited for Annie to ask what that was, but instead

Annie pointed to the FOR SALE sign in front of Great-uncle Robert's house. "When did that go up?"

"About a month ago."

Where Great-uncle Joseph's family had once lived there was now a family who kept peacocks. Annie slowed to look. "Aren't they pretty?"

"But they make weird noises. It sounds like they're saying *Help!*"

Great-uncle Samuel and Aunt Ruth still lived in their house, but they were old. Tulip mowed their yard and her dad rented their farmland. The little dollhouse was empty. Miss Doll had died two years ago at a hundred and one. The yard was overgrown inside the spiked iron fence.

"Looks like something from a spooky movie," Annie said.

Tulip nodded.

Where their great-grandparents had lived, in a house that had once been a beautiful gingerbread place that Tulip had seen in pictures, there were just the broken backs of outbuildings.

As they drove past the other farms, Tulip told Annie which neighbors had new trucks and new equipment.

"Little Miss Farmer," Annie teased.

Tulip didn't care. She thought it was interesting.

When they got to the highway, Annie shifted through the gears until they were flying. They put down the windows and turned up the radio.

At Wal-Mart, on the other side of town, they bought silk

flowers for the graves of Grandma Lovell, Great-uncle Robert, and a lot of way-back Lovells Tulip didn't know. The backseat was full of flowers when they were finished.

They were the only people at the cemetery, though a few graves had already been spruced up and decorated. They went from grave to grave, Annie sweeping away dried grass thrown up by the mowers, Tulip cleaning the monuments with a damp cloth.

It was very quiet. Big trees shaded the graves and sunlight danced over the stones in the breeze. Tulip felt the dead people waiting to be remembered.

Someone, probably Grandpa Lovell, had already put a large wreath at the base of Grandma Lovell's angel. They added a spray of silk gladiolas.

"People say she was very beautiful," Tulip said.

"And died tragically young," Annie said. "It was a great love story."

Tulip nodded. People told it the same way they told other cemetery stories. The eleven-year-old boy who'd been crushed by a piano. The man who had fathered twenty-three living children. The little girl who'd died of hydrophobia. The good doctor who'd nursed everybody through the flu epidemic of 1918, then sickened and died himself. And Belle Lovell, the beautiful bride with the handsome husband, who'd been called home to heaven too soon, leaving her heartbroken little daughter behind.

They moved on to Great-uncle Robert's grave. He'd died from cancer a few months ago.

"I think we should put lots of flowers here," Tulip said. "He probably hates being dead more than everybody else because the others have been dead a long time."

"I don't suppose he has any feeling about it one way or the other," Annie said. But she didn't discourage Tulip's plan.

They moved on to graves of the very old Lovells. At each one, as they did every year, Annie read the name and dates, and Tulip laid a few flowers on the ground in front of the marker.

Annie would probably think she was being silly, but Tulip felt the dead people's appreciation. She knew they had been waiting. She and Annie were probably the only visitors they had, the only people who still said their names.

"Why do we never say Harriet Jane's name?" she asked—not that their oldest sister was dead. She lived abroad. She'd moved away before Tulip was born.

"Because it upsets Dad," Annie said.

"Do you remember her?" Tulip asked.

Annie nodded, but her face got that closed look Tulip knew too well.

"How old were you when Harriet Jane went away?"

"I was eight and when we're done here—which we almost are—let's go to the new mall over by St. Louis. We can ask Mom if she wants to come."

That sounded boring. The only thing to recommend it was being with Annie. "Maybe," Tulip said. "But it feels wrong not to say a person's name. It's like she doesn't exist anymore. We don't have to talk about her around Dad. But you and I can talk about her."

Annie sighed. She undid the bandana around her neck and took a long time tying up her hair with it. Finally, she said, "What do you want to know?"

"Why did she leave us?"

"Do you pinky swear you'll not tell Dad I told you stuff?"

Tulip locked her finger with Annie's.

"She left—"

"Say her name. We should say her name."

Annie rolled her eyes. "Harriet Jane left when she was seventeen. She ran away."

"Why?" It was the best home in the world.

"I don't know. I was just a kid. Nobody told me anything." Annie sat down under a tree and unbuckled her platform shoes. "These shoes aren't very comfortable," she said, wiggling her toes.

Tulip sat beside her. She so hoped she looked like Annie when she grew up.

"Nobody told me anything, but I overheard a lot of stuff." Annie looked at Tulip. "You know. Grown-ups talking when they don't think you're listening."

Tulip nodded for her to go on.

"You swore you'd keep this conversation secret forever and ever." Annie raised a reminding eyebrow at Tulip.

"Yes."

"She stole her savings bonds for college out of the freezer and ran away to the West Coast and became a hippie."

"*Why?*" It was really wrong to steal. And hippies used drugs and weren't very clean.

Annie leaned her head back and stared up through the leaves. "Harriet Jane was kind of weird. It's hard to describe. She was very beautiful and very smart, but something was wrong with her."

"What?"

"Sometimes she got so sad. She tried to hide it, but you could see it in her eyes. Other times she acted so happy. Mom seemed to understand. I always thought she loved Harriet Jane most. Maybe because she was the first child, but maybe because Mom knew Harriet Jane was having a hard time. After she ran away, I heard Mom crying and trying to explain Harriet Jane to Dad, and he flew into a rage. They didn't get along for a couple of years. In front of us, they tried to act like everything was okay, but we all knew it wasn't. Mom actually left for a few months, if you can believe that. It was awful. I thought the world had ended. And Dad was so weird. He just went totally silent about Harriet Jane and Mom, like if he pretended everything was okay, then it was. And we had to pretend too. *Had* to. I knew if I failed at that, the world would truly end. I've never been so terrified."

A tear slipped down Annie's cheek. "Mom wrote to me, but the letters didn't *say* anything. Just that she loved me and wanted me to be a good girl and not be afraid. To trust our dad to take care of us. But he hadn't taken care of Harriet Jane and he hadn't taken care of Mama. I knew she was gone forever and I'd have to grow up by myself. I used to hide in the attic and cry. Phoebe and Mona had each other, but I felt like I didn't have anybody."

"You have me," Tulip said.

Annie laughed despite her tears. "I do now. But I didn't then." She wiped her face. "That's the crazy part. Nobody knew it, but Mama was pregnant with you. And I guess when you were born, she had to come home."

Annie's face was flushed. She hugged Tulip. "It was so good to have her back, to see Dad making over you and Mama, to hold sweet little you."

Tulip's heart ached. Thank goodness she'd gotten to skip that time in her family. "And then what happened?"

"We healed. We forgot. Or pretended we did."

"But what happened to Harriet Jane?"

"I don't know." Annie shook her head. "Harriet Jane was a closed subject then, and she's stayed a closed subject. Though I think she and Mama write to each other. Mama wouldn't really abandon any of her girls."

Tulip stood up, her stomach churning. The house without their mama was too terrible to think about. She wished Annie hadn't told her that.

"Let's finish up," she said. She knew she sounded mad.

"Hey," Annie said. "You asked."

"I know." But what she'd heard was worse than anything she could imagine. Their mother had left them. She tried to see it in her mind—their mama not there. It made her feel like she was falling off a skyscraper.

Annie got to her feet. She put her hands on Tulip's shoulders. "It was a hard time in our family. But we got through it. Actually, you got us through it. You made everything better. Dad adored you. He knew there wouldn't be any more kids. You were his last hope for a farmer," she said, smiling.

Tulip tried to smile back. She picked up the few flowers they had left. But her feelings got the best of her. "Why did nobody ever tell me this?" she cried.

"Because we wanted to forget the bad parts," Annie said, tucking Tulip's hair behind her ear. "About Harriet Jane running away and Mama leaving Dad."

Tulip shook her head, sending her hair back into her face. "It makes me feel left out," she said.

"And because we wanted to protect you. See how it hurts? I shouldn't have told you even now."

Tulip took a deep breath and let it out. She didn't want to talk about it. "Let's finish," she said.

As Annie read the names and dates of the last Lovells, Tulip wasn't listening. She didn't say hello to the people and feel them stir at her friendliness. She laid flowers down when Annie stopped speaking and moved to the next grave.

She listened to the birds, trying not to cry. This family Annie had told her about seemed as foreign as the postcards in Great-grandma Belle's wardrobe.

Lovell family tree

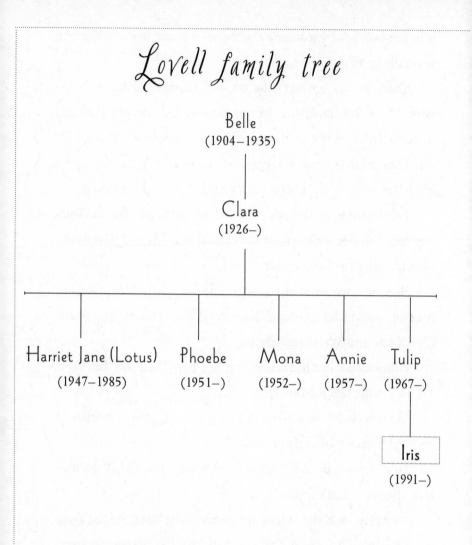

Belle
(1904–1935)

Clara
(1926–)

Harriet Jane (Lotus)
(1947–1985)

Phoebe
(1951–)

Mona
(1952–)

Annie
(1957–)

Tulip
(1967–)

Iris
(1991–)

·· five ··

Iris

2001

*I*RIS was the last kid left on the bus. She walked forward to stand by the driver. "I'm not getting off at my grandma's today. I'm getting off at home."

Miss Daley, who Iris saw every morning and afternoon of her life, as regular as sunrise and sunset, met Iris's eyes in the mirror. "I hope Clara isn't sick."

"No. She's fine. I have a dentist appointment, and my dad is waiting at home to take me."

"Is he home for the summer?"

Iris nodded. Her dad was a college professor. Usually he was just home weekends, except in the summer, when he was home all the time and he and her mom fought a lot.

"Will Annie be coming to visit anytime soon?" Miss Daley asked. She and Aunt Annie had been friends in high school. Aunt Annie lived in Portland now. She was a doctor.

"Maybe. I don't really know."

"Well, you tell her hi for me if you see her, okay?"

Iris nodded.

When the bus stopped at the end of the drive, Iris said, "Bye!"

"See you tomorrow. Same time, same place." Miss Daley said that every afternoon.

It seemed strange to be dropped off at home. Normally, Grandma Clara was waiting at the dollhouse, acting as if Iris was the high point of her day.

Iris opened the mailbox at the end of the drive, hoping there might be an envelope with her name on it. She had a birthday next week and sometimes cards from the aunts came early, and they had money inside. But there was just boring stuff addressed to Tulip Smith or Lawrence Smith, her parents.

Iris cut across the grass to the front door. She was surprised the house was closed up, since it was such a pretty day.

The front door was locked.

She rang the doorbell and waited. And waited, a lump growing in her throat.

Finally, she tilted the flowerpot where the secret key was kept. It wasn't there.

She pressed the doorbell again, knowing she was acting pathetic but longing to hear the sound of her dad's footsteps, wanting him to open the door, wanting him to say if they hurried, they could still get to the appointment on time.

The clock inside bonged four o'clock.

Leaving her book bag in the porch swing, she went to the north end of the house and peered through the garage window. Both her parents' cars were gone.

They had forgotten her.

Tears burning her eyes, she sat in the porch swing and stared at nothing. Her ears ached, listening for the sound of a car. She looked down the road, hoping to see one of her parents' cars turn the corner at the cemetery.

People got in car accidents. They also had heart attacks, choked on food, and drowned. Lots of things could kill people. Bees, snakes, tornadoes.

Crows cawed angrily from behind the house. They made her think of her parents when she lay on the floor by the secret listening post under her bed, where she could hear every word, where she could even hear her dad lift the cap off a bottle of beer. She could hear her mother sigh.

Didn't they ever wonder where she was and what she was doing when she was up there with her ear pressed to the opening behind the baseboard?

Sometimes they liked each other. Her dad enjoyed cooking for them on the weekends. Sometimes, though, he cooked fancy stuff that they mispronounced and he tried to hide his smile, but her mother always saw it and got mad. Sometimes her dad was funny and made her mother laugh. Sometimes he seemed proud she ran a big farm, and sometimes she seemed proud he wrote books. Her mother had conservation awards on the wall behind her desk in the office they shared. Her dad had two books he'd written on the bookshelf behind his desk. But they said mean things to each other. Her dad said her mother was letting herself go. Where was the beauty queen he'd married? Her mother said her dad better look out for that wandering eye of his. It had gotten him in trouble before.

The clock inside chimed four thirty. She wasn't going to wait any longer. She stood up, put her book bag over her shoulder, and began to walk.

It felt like a long way to Grandma Clara's house. She turned east at the corner, going up the first hill. The grazing cows and calves raised their heads and looked at her.

The sky seemed really high and the barn far away, as if the world had gotten bigger or she had gotten smaller. Nobody knew where she was. What if somebody came along and tried to kidnap her? They probably wouldn't. But they might.

If she heard a car, she'd run to the bridge, scramble down the bank, and hide in the water. But she didn't hear a car. Or anything.

There was only one house along this road and a big dog lived there. She saw him standing at attention on the front porch. She looked straight ahead and walked as if she were invisible, barely breathing. She counted backward from a hundred by threes, telling herself if she just kept counting, the dog wouldn't be able to move. She didn't look, not even out of the corner of her eye. Her heart was racing but she didn't rush.

When she was well past, she relaxed and walked faster.

Eventually she got to the dollhouse. It looked different—lonely—without Grandma Clara standing on the porch waiting for her. She went through the squeaky metal gate.

"Grandma Clara?"

Maybe she wasn't home either.

"Anybody home?" Iris cried, her voice shaking.

Finally, she heard her grandmother's voice. "Iris?"

"Yes! I'm here."

Her grandmother came to the door and opened it. "What are you doing here?" She looked sleepy. She didn't quite have her welcoming face on. "I was having a nap," she said.

Iris felt her face breaking up.

"Oh, you poor girl," Grandma Clara said, folding Iris in her arms. "What's wrong?"

"There's nobody home at our house."

Her grandmother put her arm around Iris's shoulder and steered her inside. "Something got mixed up, didn't it?"

Iris swallowed and nodded, embarrassed she'd almost cried like a baby.

"Well, I was missing you. That's why I took a nap. Wash your hands while I make our snack."

The familiar smell of the soap in the tiny bathroom made Iris feel a million times better. She looked in the mirror over the sink. She wished she didn't have freckles, but she felt better about them when her grandmother called them *Annie's freckles*. She liked her aunt Annie.

At the round table in front of the window, Grandma Clara laid down pretty cloth napkins, which always made Iris feel like a princess. When the English muffins popped out of the toaster,

Iris buttered them and spread them with strawberry jam they'd made last summer. Grandma Clara poured Iris a glass of milk and herself a glass of water, and they sat at the table eating.

Iris felt much better. She could see their house across the field. The sky didn't look so big now.

"I wish you lived in our house," she said. "Like you used to when Mom was little. Why don't you? We have lots of room."

"A house can use only one mistress at a time," Grandma Clara said.

Iris didn't know for sure what that meant.

"And I'm the mistress of this house now and happy as a bed-bug. Tulip is the mistress of that house."

"But she's not happy as a bedbug."

Grandma Clara waited to see if Iris had more to say.

But she didn't. She didn't want her grandmother to know what life was like at her house. How unimportant Iris was.

Grandma Clara finally said, "Families say and do terrible things to each other, Iris. It shouldn't be that way, but it is. Usually, everything works out okay in the end. And I'm always right here."

"I know." Iris couldn't bear to think about life without the dollhouse and her grandmother inside.

After they finished eating, her grandmother called and left a message for Iris's parents that apparently there'd been a mix-up and Iris was with her.

Then they went onto the sleeping porch, which Grandma

Clara also used as a sewing room. There were chairs for both of them and a worktable and the sewing machine and the hope chest Grandma Clara's grandfather had made when Grandma Clara was ten.

Every time Grandma Clara opened the hope chest, Iris saw treasure. Not silver and gold and jewels, but a great trove of fabric remnants, buttons, yarn, thread, ricrac, lace, piping, needles, and stuffing, which they used to fashion their dolls.

Grandma Clara was looking at Iris, a smile forming. "You know what?" Grandma Clara asked.

Iris shook her head.

"When I'm gone, you should have my hope chest."

The thought of Grandma Clara being gone stabbed Rose.

"But that won't be for a long time," Grandma Clara said, hugging Iris and getting out their project.

The doll they'd been working on for several days was almost done. They had a process for all their dolls. First, Iris wrote down five things about the doll they were going to make. The one she was working on now was eleven years old, longed for a twin sister, had a horse she rode everywhere—even to the mailbox and the garden—was good at keeping secrets, and wanted to grow up and be a wedding planner.

Then Grandma Clara cut the doll's shape, front and back, out of skin-colored, stretchy fabric. They stitched the front to the back, leaving an opening for the stuffing, and turned it inside out so the seams didn't show. And then they stuffed it and closed the opening. They nipped and tucked with hand stitches to make cheeks and chin and personality. They put on the faces with paint and markers. Sometimes for the eyes, they glued bits of paper. If the doll was a boy, they usually painted the hair. Otherwise they made yarn hair. Iris loved making the clothing and accessories.

Now and then, the dolls didn't really look like what Iris had in mind when she wrote five things about them. If the girl they were working on now didn't end up looking cheerful enough to be a wedding planner, Grandma Clara would say—as she always did—that real people sometimes didn't turn out like you expected them to either.

Iris took some of the dolls home with her. Some she left with her grandmother, who kept them lined up on a shelf like trophies.

Iris was making sunglasses out of heavy paper and plastic wrap and glue. Anyone who rode a horse a lot and wanted to be a wedding planner someday would have sunglasses. Grandma Clara was telling family stories, as she often did on their after-school afternoons. Iris liked it when her grandmother did that, even though Iris wasn't always totally listening. But she still liked her grandmother's calm voice talking about people who were old or dead now but had once been kids. About times when electricity or bathrooms or televisions or computers hadn't been invented.

". . . in those days, I was a young mother still having babies and I expected so much out of Harriet Jane. We all did. She was a tall girl, like you. Maybe that's why. I expected much less of Phoebe and Mona. And Annie, our baby, I spoiled silly."

"But my mom was the baby," Iris reminded her gently. Sometimes Grandma Clara got mixed up.

"Ummm," Grandma Clara said, licking the tip of thread so it would go through a needle more easily, "she was Harriet Jane's baby."

Iris stared at her grandmother. Grandma Clara looked as if she might like to take her words back. But then she lifted one shoulder in a shrug. "Everybody in the family knows, but we don't talk about it. It's a secret."

"I'm good at keeping secrets."

"I know you are, sweetheart," Grandma Clara said.

Clara felt warm inside that Grandma Clara was trusting her. But she also felt dizzy from this astonishing information.

"But why did you pretend she was your daughter?" Iris asked.

"In those days, Harriet Jane was a wild thing off in San Francisco. And my husband, Ralph, couldn't deal with the way she was living. Ralph didn't bend in the wind, which is probably what killed him. And when she changed her name from Harriet Jane Hoffmann, his good family name, to Lotus Lovell—what she called her flower child name—that was the absolute end."

Grandma Clara went on. "She was going to have a baby but didn't have a husband. People don't care much about that now, but they did then. Ralph especially didn't want anybody to know. We both loved children and hadn't had one for ten years and thought all that was behind us. And it just seemed the best for everybody because Harriet Jane was beginning her life and maybe not really meant to be a mother. So I went to live with her in California for five months and came home with a baby and let everybody think she was our late-life child. Those things do happen. It was an awfully hard time for the family. Phoebe and Mona knew what was going on, though we kept it from little Annie. She was too young to understand."

Iris was struggling to take this in. It was the most grown-up thing anybody had ever talked to her about. She thought of Harriet Jane as a superstar who had become famous for her prints of people holding bouquets and for saving the Lovell land during the farm crisis.

Plus, all this meant Grandma Clara wasn't who Iris had always thought she was. "You're really my great-grandmother," she said.

"Well, I guess I am," Grandma Clara said, as if she hadn't thought of that before and it didn't make a stitch of difference. "But what I'm trying to explain is that for most of us, life is long. We like to think we know how someone is going to turn out. But we don't. So we shouldn't give up on people. We shouldn't give up on ourselves either."

Grandma Clara began to sew little buttons on the jacket of the doll who was going to be a wedding planner someday. Iris put the finishing touches on the sunglasses.

Before long, she heard the sound of her dad's Jeep coming up the road.

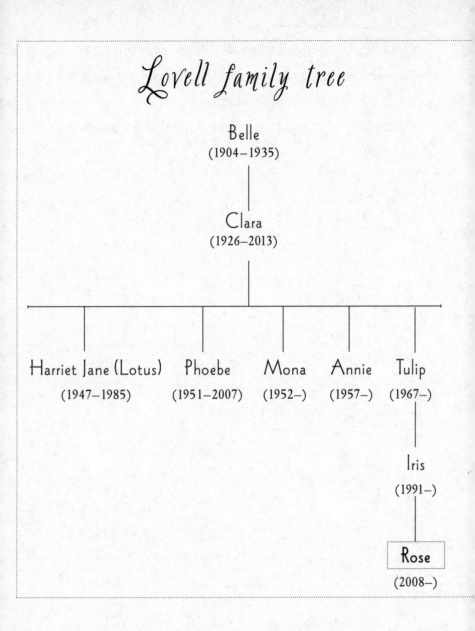

Lovell family tree

Belle
(1904–1935)

Clara
(1926–2013)

Harriet Jane (Lotus)
(1947–1985)

Phoebe
(1951–2007)

Mona
(1952–)

Annie
(1957–)

Tulip
(1967–)

Iris
(1991–)

Rose
(2008–)

six

Rose

AT the end of the day, Ama was late picking her up at school. Both buses had already pulled out, and the last car in the pickup line was gone. The flag ruffled in the breeze. The long dress and love beads were hot, and Rose was thirsty. But Ama would be here. Ama would never forget her.

When the dusty farm truck finally crunched gravel in the school parking lot, Rose jumped up and ran to get in. Myrtle gave her a quick kiss as she climbed into the seat.

"Sorry," Ama said. "The car died on the way here and I had to walk home for the truck." Ama looked dirty and sweaty from the hayfield. She also looked rushed. "How did the report go?"

"Fine. Everybody thought Lotus was beautiful and talented. And they thought it was cool that we have flower names because she saved the farm. And the teacher praised me for talking about important times like the hippie era, the Vietnam War, and the farm crisis. But she did think it was weird the family tree didn't have any men on it."

Ama laughed, a deep head-thrown-back laugh. "We only had so much room on the paper," she said.

"I know." Rose laughed too as if she got the joke, though she wasn't sure she did.

Ama had the windows lowered, and the wind blowing Rose's hair felt nice. She slid down in the seat and shut her eyes. The report was behind her. She felt free to just be.

She knew every hill, curve, and pothole on the way home. She figured she'd traveled the six miles between home and school approximately three thousand times. Although her eyes were closed, she knew when they passed the Youngs' because she smelled their lilacs. She knew when they were about to turn onto Goldenrod Lane because of the *bump-bump-bump* right before Ama braked for the turn. She waited for the dip in the road in front of the bright blue house where the goats lived.

"There's the car," Ama said, braking.

Rose opened her eyes. The car was half in the ditch where Ama had left it.

"I have jumpers in the back. If it will start, can you drive it home?"

Rose sat up. *"Me?"*

"You drove the harvest truck a little last fall," Ama reminded her. "And you drove the tractor through the gate just last week."

Ama always made Rose feel as if she could do anything.

"I need to get back to the hayfield. Now they're saying rain on Friday. Besides, it's only two miles. And we'll probably be the only people on the road."

A lot could go wrong in two miles. What if she ran over the beagle that always charged into the road, barking and snarling and trying to bite the tires?

Maybe the car wouldn't start.

But it did.

Ama disconnected the jumper cables, slammed the hood, and tossed the cables in the back of the truck.

"I'll turn the car around for you and point it the right way, then all you need to do is follow."

When Rose was in the driver's seat, boosted by her book bag so she could see out the windshield and reach the pedals, she gripped the steering wheel. Ama squeezed Rose's shoulder. "Don't worry. We'll creep along. Keep about four car lengths between us."

What if somebody came up behind them and honked? Rose would feel stupid.

Ama turned on the car's emergency flashers. "If anybody gets behind us, which they probably won't, they'll know we have to drive slow. Now put your foot on the brake and put the car in drive."

Rose knew how because she had watched Ama do it hundreds of times. Rose squeezed the gearshift and steering wheel to stop her hands from trembling. When she moved the gearshift from P to D, the car felt like a charging rhino—something too big and wild and dangerous for her to control. She clenched her jaw.

Rose and her cousin Maddy had a Brave Girls Club and made each other do crazy stunts, but nothing like this.

Rose's leg shook as she eased off the brake.

They crawled along the narrow gravel road crowded by fencerows. When they passed the house with the beagle, he lay on the porch. He stood up and looked at them, then sank back down. They weren't going fast enough to chase.

On the first curve, Rose didn't slow down quite enough and left wet, sweaty handprints on the steering wheel when she was finally going straight again.

Before the next big curve, Ama's arm came out the window, warning Rose to start slowing sooner. But Rose didn't turn the wheel enough and the car dipped into the ditch. Her cheeks flamed as weeds scraped along the underside. When she steered the car out of the ditch, Ama flashed a thumbs-up.

Only one turn left.

And Rose did it fine. Ama tapped her horn in a little cheer.

When they could see the house straight ahead, Ama speeded up, and so did Rose.

Finally parked in the driveway, Ama got out of the truck and strode back to the car.

Rose got out on shaking legs. Her heart was way up between her ears and trying to jump out.

"Homeric!" Ama said, high-fiving Rose.

Ama hardly ever said that.

"Well done!" Ama squeezed Rose's shoulders and kissed

the top of her head when she got out of the car. "You were a brave kid."

Myrtle had leapt out of the truck and was kissing Rose's fingers and wagging her tail. Giddy from driving on the road, Rose had a great idea. "May I move today?"

Moving day was always the last day of school, and there were still two weeks left.

Ama's eyebrows rose, but she said, "I don't see why not. Do you know where you're going?"

"Yes." Rose grinned. There was really only one place left to go and Ama knew it.

"But I can't help you until later," Ama said. "I have to finish cutting."

"I know. I'll get started, and we can finish when you come in."

Ama gave her another hug. "Thanks for helping with the car." She walked away, then turned back. "If I'm not in by dusk, would you check the chickens' feed and water?"

"Sure."

Rose gathered up her book bag and went inside. She'd already slept in three of the upstairs bedrooms. She thought she was ready for the last one.

Until she started kindergarten, her bedroom had been downstairs, across the hall from Ama's—so close Rose could hear Ama's nice, cozy snore. That tiny bedroom had been like a baby's room. Like it was for someone who might need her mommy or grandma in the night. And Rose didn't after she started kindergarten. And what was the point of a big house if you didn't live in all of it?

Ama and her sisters had slept upstairs when they were girls. The backsides of the closet doors still showed the horizontal marks that measured their heights. So far, Rose had slept in Annie's, Mona's, and Phoebe's rooms. It felt right, after all that had happened today, for Rose to move into the room that been first Harriet Jane's, then Ama's.

She knew every alcove and hidey-hole of the upstairs. Every squeaky board and listening post. Ama almost never came up here. It was Rose's world. When she was little and still played with dolls, she'd spread them out among the bedrooms and visited them as if going house to house.

Some of the dolls had belonged to the Greats, or to Ama and her sisters, or to Rose's mother, Iris. The ones from the Greats had glass heads and limbs, and they smelled musty. Some had hard, shiny plastic faces and hair. Ama's dolls talked in annoying voices when you pulled strings on their backs. Iris's dolls were weird.

Rose had found them in a closet, in a box labeled IRIS. When Rose asked Ama if Iris had actually played with them, Ama had shrugged, looking like she didn't know what to say. She explained that Iris and Grandma Clara had made the dolls when Iris was young. They weren't cuddly like Rose's own dolls, who liked to be wrapped in blankets and rocked and fed and changed when they were wet. But her mother's dolls looked as if they had stories inside them. Rose had sensed that Ama wanted to say *Why don't you put those back where you found them, Rose?* But Ama didn't say that, so Rose had introduced them to her other dolls when Ama wasn't around.

Not long after, Rose had decided she was too old for dolls. Except for her mother's, she stored them in the empty wardrobe at the end of the hall. That seemed more respectful than just cramming them in the attic. The wardrobe was very old and very beautiful and the drawers were painted a glossy red on the inside. Rose looked in on the dolls in their retirement home now and then.

She kept her mother's dolls in her glass-fronted bookcase. She wasn't sure why. She remembered seeing Iris only once in her whole life. It was one of her first memories and not very clear. But it didn't matter because she didn't care a thing about her mother. Life with Ama was perfect.

In her old room, she threw open the windows. Although the hayfield was beyond the barn, the smell of freshly mown hay rode in on the breeze.

She changed out of the hippie costume and into shorts and a T-shirt. After putting her head under the faucet to wash out the fake waves, she brushed her hair back into her usual ponytail, glad to look like herself again.

Standing in the middle of her new room, she planned where things would go. This room was the biggest of the upstairs bedrooms. The south window gave her a view across the field to the cemetery, where she could see Great-great-grandma Belle's angel. Beyond the cemetery was a woods. Through the west windows, she could see a long way across a field to another woods. She loved the old rose-patterned wallpaper and the wood floors aged almost to chocolate.

One of the Greats had been a lawyer. His legal bookcase, with its glass-fronted shelves, was perfect for storing Rose's art supplies and her mother's dolls. She unloaded everything into a box. The bookcase came apart into five sections, and Rose could carry each one by herself. In her new room, she put the bookcase back together.

Her art supplies were pages she ripped out of catalogues and magazines, used wrapping paper, decorative paper sacks. Antique beads and buttons saved by the Greats. Feathers, rocks, and leaves she picked up. But she also had paints, brushes, markers, and origami folding tools. Glue, scissors, rulers, and books. She put those things on the top two shelves.

On the bottom shelf, she arranged Iris's dolls, studying them as she handled them. Her mother might have been about Rose's own age when she and Grandma Clara made them. Maybe her mother and Grandma Clara had loved each other a lot, just like Rose and Ama loved each other.

The antique wooden wheels of the camelback trunk squeaked and squealed as Rose rolled it across the hall. A girl named Dora Hoffmann had brought the trunk from Germany, and it came into this house when Great-grandpa Hoffmann married Great-grandma Clara. Inside, along with Rose's things, were a framed picture of the family Dora had left behind in Düsseldorf and a long-handled silver spoon, tarnished but fancy.

Then, tilting and turning it to get it through the doors, Rose slid her comfy chair across the hall and into her new room to sit in front of the south window. By turning her desk on its side, she was able to scoot it through the doors too. Then came her desk chair, bulletin board, and lamp—which was all of the furniture except her bed. Ama would have to help with that. Rose decided not to move the big chest of drawers because the closet in her new room had shelves for her clothes.

But before she did anything else, she should take care of Peanutbutter and the chickens.

#

She wasn't surprised to see the Wyandottes outside the pen because they were escape artists. Noisy, always-clucking little escape artists. Last February, when the farm had been frozen and brown and quiet and there wasn't a lot to do except feed the cattle and keep their water open, she and Ama had gone chicken shopping. Chickens for a few eggs, Ama said. Chickens for fun.

They'd bought two rainbow pullets, which laid pretty pastel eggs; two Barred Rocks, which made Rose think of salt and pepper shakers; two Sienna Stars, which made her think of the sunset; two Golden Laced Wyandottes, which were so beautiful

67

they didn't even look real; and two California Whites, which Ama said were sensible white chickens for an otherwise crazy flock. And they bought a fancy little chicken house, which her Cousin Maddy called the Palace.

Rose scooped up the Wyandottes and put them in the pen. Then she checked the feeder and filled the water tank.

When she got to the barn, she heard the tractor in the distance. She couldn't see it because it was over the rise. But the hayfield lay flat on the ground except for the little patch close to the barn. The smell of new-mown hay hung in the air.

Rose mixed the formula at the sink in the shop and took it to the pen. Peanutbutter frisked around, bumping the bottle before she began to suck with a blissful look in her eyes.

"You're such a good girl," Rose said, rubbing under her chin. "Such a pretty girl."

When the bottle was empty, Rose tied up Peanutbutter. Although she'd been doing it morning and night for a while, it made her stomach feel funny every time. Ama said it didn't hurt Peanutbutter one bit, although Peanutbutter always fought the rope at first. When she settled down, Rose brushed her and talked to her.

She left the calf tied while she cleaned out the straw and replaced it with fresh. She weighed calf starter into the food bucket, washed the water pail, and refilled it. Then she squeezed an oral gel into Peanutbutter's mouth because she was drinking city water while she was in the pen. The vet said the chemicals in the water killed bacteria cows need in their digestive system, and the gel had probiotics in it.

Leaving Peanutbutter tied, Rose did her record-keeping, writing in the binder that hung outside the stall door. At the fair, her records about her calf would be the most important part of the judging. The records would show Peanutbutter's weight gain, what Rose had fed her the first ninety days, what Rose had fed her the next ninety days, how much it had cost to feed and care for her, what equipment Rose had used, how many times the vet had visited and what he'd done. Last week, he'd come to treat the best bull for pinkeye, and while he was there, he'd taken a look at Peanutbutter and said she was a fine little heifer. Rose had written that in the binder. *A fine little heifer.* The words made her feel proud.

The sound of the tractor came closer. Rose hoped Ama had finished all she wanted to get done.

Inside the stall, Peanutbutter was standing quietly. Rose cuddled her and unhooked the rope, setting her free to gallop around the pen.

"See you tomorrow," Rose said. "Bright and early."

She and Ama and Myrtle walked to the house together. The shadows were long and the dropping sun stretched pink fingers across the sky.

"Did you finish?" Rose said.

"Yes. It's a great first cutting." Ama sounded tired and happy.

\#

After dinner, when it was fully dark and the chickens had gone to roost, Ama and Myrtle went out to shut the henhouse door and Rose went upstairs.

Ama came up before long, Myrtle at her heels. When she saw what Rose had done, she said, "Wow! Looks like you don't need much help."

"Just the bed."

They moved the mattress and springs, then took the bed apart and carried the frame, headboard, and footboard into Rose's new room.

Rose held the pieces of the bed frame in place while Ama tightened the bolts. Ama's hands were always banged up from farmwork, but they felt as soft as Myrtle's ears when Ama trimmed Rose's bangs and evened up the ragged ends of her ponytail.

"So why are you moving early?" Ama asked.

Ama said bragging made a person as boring as a fencepost. But still. "I *did* drive the car home." Rose broke out in a huge smile. "And I think that means I might be mature enough to move into your old room." And despite nearly dying of stage fright, she'd given a good oral report. Her hands had shaken so much she'd had to put the note cards down, but the memorized words had poured back into her head.

When the springs and mattress were seated on the bed frame, Ama said, "There. That's done." She looked around. "When we hung this wallpaper, I was fifteen, and these roses were bright red." She laughed. "See me now. And see these faded roses. They're barely even pink."

"But they're still pretty," Rose said. Ama was pretty too. She had been an official beauty queen.

"I'll leave you to finish," Ama said.

Ama went downstairs, Myrtle following at her heels. Myrtle loved Rose, but Myrtle was a work dog, and Ama was the person who understood what work needed to be done.

Rose made her bed and rehung her shadow boxes in the new room. Night bugs tapped against the screens as she worked. There were three shadow boxes. Her favorite was the Bottle Calf. She always capitalized him in her head because he was meant to capture the spirit of all the calves whose mamas couldn't or wouldn't take care of them, so Ama and Rose had to. Over the years, bottle calves had come in all colors—black, cream, reddish, brownish. One had looked pink in the right light. One was patterned like a jigsaw puzzle. The Bottle Calf in the shadow box was folded out of brown paper and she hoped he looked both needy and feisty, which bottle calves almost always were. And bottle calves had sweet faces and eyes that made you love them even though they were a ton of trouble. She hoped she'd captured that.

Another was of her and Ama and Myrtle walking toward the barn on a summer day. And one was of the night sky showing the Big Dipper and the Little Dipper and the bright polestar at the tip of the Little Dipper's handle. A tiny shadowy figure, who Rose intended to be herself, looked up, trying to find the polestar.

When the shadow boxes were hung in a row, she stowed her shorts, jeans, shirts, socks, pajamas, and panties on the shelves in the closet. She didn't have bras yet, though her cousin Maddy did.

Rose unpacked her schoolwork, putting the visuals from her report in a folder and labeling it ORAL REPORT, 4TH GRADE, and placed it in the trunk along with other important papers. The only things she kept out were the photo of Lotus and the family tree.

Rose pinned them to her bulletin board. Then, in the lamplight, she turned slowly, taking in her new space. On the north wall were her desk, bookcase, and bulletin board. On the west wall were two big windows with the camelback trunk between them. On the south was another large window with Rose's comfy chair in front of it. On the east were two doors, one to the closet and one to the hall. In the empty space of the east wall were the shadow boxes. And in the center of the room was Rose's bed.

None of the windows had curtains because nobody could see her upstairs in the middle of the country except birds and squirrels. The night air smelled cool and damp.

Rose turned off the lamp to make the bugs go away, then went downstairs. Ama heard her coming and got out the three little fancy fluted bowls left by the Greats and filled them with strawberry sherbet. Myrtle's bowl drummed against the baseboard as she licked.

When they were finished, they went into Ama's bedroom. Myrtle curled up in her dog bed and Ama sank into her chair. Rose stood behind her. Rose brushed Ama's hair every night because Ama had a bad shoulder from years of steering the tractor.

As Rose brushed Ama's thick, honey-colored hair streaked with gray, she counted the strokes to one hundred. Ama's hair crackled like a little fire that warmed Rose. Then Rose sat on the floor in front of Ama. Ama gently slipped Rose's ponytail free and her hair fell around her shoulders. Every night, that was a delicious feeling that lasted only an eyeblink. One Rose looked forward to. And then Ama began to brush.

That was how every day ended. And as Ama brushed a hundred strokes, such love and happiness and contentment welled up in Rose she wished they could die together in that moment. Not that she wanted to die, but they loved each other so much that she wanted them to die *together*.

··seven··

THE first morning of summer vacation, Rose pressed the pillow over her ears to blot out the bawling of the poor little weaners. Ama had separated the fall calves from their mamas yesterday. In a few days the calves would be perfectly happy eating delicious fresh pasture, but now they wanted their mamas' warm milk.

Rose flung back the covers.

Downstairs, Ama was at the kitchen table working on her laptop. "You're up early for summer vacation."

Rose poured a little coffee and a lot of milk into a mug. She wondered if she loved coffee because Ama smelled like coffee.

"Maddy will be here shortly," Ama said.

Maddy was staying with them for a couple of days while Uncle Thomas and Aunt Carol were at a medical convention. They weren't really Rose's aunt and uncle. She just called them that. Uncle Thomas, Great-aunt Phoebe's son, was really Ama's nephew, though he was about Ama's age. And Maddy was Rose's best friend.

"You girls can help me move fencing this morning if you want to."

Rose wanted to because she knew it would make the job go much faster for Ama. "Sure," she said. But while Maddy liked picking bluebells and hunting mushrooms and wading in the creek, Rose didn't know how Maddy would feel about being out in the pasture with big animals and cow poop everywhere and actually working.

A while later, Rose and Maddy were squeezed behind Ama on the four-wheeler, bouncing across the pasture pulling a wagon, with Myrtle running along beside them. Rose hopped off to open and close gates until they got to the fence they were going to move.

Maddy lasted about ten minutes. She was getting sunburned on her nose and shoulders. She could feel it. She had stepped in cow poop. She could smell it. The grass was making her itch. She was thirsty. She needed to go to the bathroom. She was b-o-r-e-d.

Finally, Ama got fed up. "If you girls would rather go to the house, Myrtle and I can finish this alone. But basic rules. Use good sense. And stay together. Okay?"

"Sure!" Maddy said, cheering up.

They walked home through the big round hay bales, golden green in the sun.

Maddy said, "Poor you. Stuck out here all the time with nothing to do."

"Nothing to do?"

Maddy didn't have a dog or a bottle calf. Maddy never heard

coyotes or whippoorwills. She never got to watch the big bull snake prowling the hay barn looking for mice. Never got to see the raccoon, with his rippling fur and bandit eyes, slink out of the old linden in the dusk to begin his day. She didn't have hay bales.

"Well, guess what I'm doing," Maddy said. "I'm taking a babysitting class. I've learned the Heimlich maneuver and CPR—skills that will look good on my resume now that I'm eleven and old enough to start a babysitting business."

Rose had learned the Heimlich maneuver in 4-H, but not CPR.

As they got close to the barn, the weaners were bawling so loudly Maddy put her hands over her ears. "What's wrong with them, anyway?"

"They want their mamas. But they need to start eating pasture. Ama's weaning them."

"That's so mean!"

"No, it isn't! What if your mom was still nursing you?"

"Eww! Please!" Then Maddy said, "Why are your cows different colors? Some people have all black cows."

Their neighbor to the west had a big operation of Angus. Maddy had probably seen them on the way to the farm. They were beautiful animals—shiny black against the green pasture.

"Ama says crossbreed cattle are better in a herd our size."

"So how big is your herd?"

Rose shrugged as if she didn't know, because the question

was personal and a little bit rude. But Ama tried to keep it around a hundred.

#

Later, when Ama came in, they made lunch; then they got in the truck and went to the dollhouse so Ama could measure for carpet. After Great-grandma Clara died, Ama had rented the house to a man who had recently moved to Missouri to be near his children. Ama was going to spruce it up before she advertised it for rent again.

When Ama found the key under a brick and unlocked the door, the house let out a stuffy sigh. Inside, the row of stained-glass squares decorated the tops of the kitchen windows and threw bits of colored light around the room.

"I remember coming here to visit Great-grandma," Rose said. "I think."

"You might. You were five when she died. You were her sunshine at the end of her life," Ama told Rose, touching her hair. "Mom loved kids."

While Ama measured, Rose showed Maddy around, though there was nothing to see in a small, empty house.

"Want to see naked ladies?" Rose asked.

Maddy glanced at Ama.

"Come on," Rose said, motioning and leading the way outside.

Along the south side of the garden shed, she pointed to a clump of droopy foliage.

Maddy looked confused. "Where?"

"You're looking at them."

"Oh, you're just being dumb."

"Nope. These leaves are dying back. In a few weeks, there will be nothing here. Nothing at all. Then *voilà!* Naked ladies will pop up in August."

Maddy narrowed her eyes.

"True," Ama said, coming up behind them. "But they're more politely called surprise lilies, because they surprise you."

"Then why did Rose call them naked ladies?"

Ama laughed. "Well, they're not wearing a stitch of foliage when they come back. That's the naked part. And they're pretty pink blossoms. Like ladies. My mom called them resurrection lilies. She planted them. They're my favorite flower."

Ama stood for a minute, her face tilted to the sun, her eyes closed, looking both sad and happy. Rose would have put her arm around Ama's waist and leaned against her side if Maddy hadn't been there.

As they drove to the Amish store on the highway, Ama pointed out to Maddy where Lovells had lived. She named the brothers who had farmed and raised their families along this road almost a hundred years ago. Maddy nodded, although she had heard it before. Ama drove slowly, looking at the cows in the pasture, who raised their heads from grazing to look at the truck.

At the store, they bought chicken feed, minerals for the cattle, calf starter, and formula mix. The clearance counter before checkout was crowded with marked-down climbing roses.

"Those have seen better days," Ama said. "But do you want to try planting one on the garden fence?"

"Sure," Rose said.

At home, Ama dropped the girls off at the garden and went on to the barn. Rose got the planting tools out of the garden shed.

The garden was small because Ama was so busy. Some beef farmers hired help, but Ama tried not to do that very often. Uncle Thomas came out to drive the silage wagon when he could. Otherwise, Ama paid a neighbor boy for a few days' work each August.

"I want to dig the hole," Maddy said, taking the shovel.

Rose liked to dig holes too, but Maddy was company.

While Maddy dug, Rose pumped a bucket of water. The well had been here since the first Lovells hired a water witch to find water and he tapped into an underground stream. A nice artesian well had been theirs ever since. Ama had replaced the pump so it didn't screech and squeal. And they still used it for small watering projects like planting.

Ama came into the garden with a basket just as they were finishing watering in the rose. She harvested radishes and a few handfuls of baby kale.

"Do you girls want to pick the peas?" she asked.

For every few peas she dropped in the basket, Rose popped one in her mouth. Maddy frowned.

"What?" Rose said.

"What if a bird has pooped on it?"

Rose shrugged. Nothing was finer than a pea straight from the vine to her mouth.

Late in the day, Rose and Maddy walked to the barn to feed the calf. The weaners were quieter now, worn out from their long day of bawling.

"Why does this calf get a bottle and those other calves don't?" Maddy asked.

"Those other calves are fall calves. Peanutbutter is a spring calf, and it's not time to wean her yet. Plus, those other calves have mothers who nursed them until they got big and strong enough to eat grass. They just don't want to because they're kind of spoiled. Peanutbutter's mama wouldn't claim her, so she'd starve if we didn't bottle-feed her."

"Did her mother die in childbirth?"

Rose laughed.

"What?" Maddy demanded.

"You're such a town girl."

"And proud of it," Maddy said. "You're such a redneck."

"And proud of it." But she explained farm life to her cousin. "When a cow won't claim her calf, it means she's not a good mother. And if a cow isn't a good mother, it makes for extra cost and work. So she went to the sale barn."

"That's so *mean*! Somebody probably ate her."

"It's not mean. It's how a farm works."

And that was twice today Maddy had called Ama mean.

"Ama is an excellent midwife if an animal needs help. I've helped her pull calves."

"What's pull calves?"

"Sometimes they won't come out on their own. So we pull them out."

Maddy clapped her hand over her mouth and faked throwing up. In fact, Rose had watched with terror and disgust, and Ama never did it if she could get the vet in time.

Rose made the bottle in the shop, and they found Peanutbutter with her head poking between the railings of the gate. The way she looked up through her long lashes made Rose want to kiss her topknot.

"You want to feed her?" she asked.

Maddy nodded.

"She's rowdy. She'll try to jerk the bottle out of your hand. And if she pulls the nipple off we'll have to go back to the shop and start all over. And we'll have wasted expensive formula. So hold it like this." She demonstrated.

As Peanutbutter sucked, Maddy kept a tight grip on the bottle. When it was was empty, Rose tied up Peanutbutter.

"What are you doing? You're hurting her!" Maddy said as Peanutbutter tossed her head and yanked back against the rope. "She'll choke!"

Rose shooed Maddy out of the stall. "No, she won't. It's part of her training."

While Maddy fretted, Rose did her cleaning and record-keeping. Then she petted and talked to Peanutbutter, untied her, and offered her a handful of pellets. When she was done, she asked Maddy if she'd like to feed Peanutbutter a handful.

Maddy looked doubtful and shook her head.

Lightning swelled and thunder rumbled.

"Good night," Rose told the calf. "Don't worry about the storm. Ama says it's not supposed to amount to much and we'll have a nice day tomorrow."

As they lay in bed that night after the storm had passed, Rose teetered on the edge of sleep.

"What's that?" Maddy demanded, jarring Rose back to wakefulness.

"What?"

"Sounds like a choir."

Rose sat up to listen. "Frogs. They're courting." The rain had stopped and stars blazed through her window.

"How romantic," Maddy said. "Did I tell you Tommy Cross tried to kiss me on the playground?"

"Why?"

"Because he likes me. Mama says not to pay too much attention to all that just yet. She says . . ."

Maddy's voice sounded different in the dark. Deeper. Mysterious. Mature.

"Maddy?"

"What?"

"You don't sound like yourself in the dark. Do I sound different?"

"Kind of," Maddy said. "I wonder why."

"Maybe because we can't see each other?"

"Maybe," Maddy said.

Rose lay there, Maddy's elbow in her ribs. Now she was wide awake, the music of the frogs loud. The stars were so bright she blinked her eyes. She got up and went to the south window.

"What are you doing?" Maddy said. She got out of bed and padded to the window and stood beside Rose. "What are you looking at?"

There was a breeze. There were a moon and starlight. It was on nights like these that the angel sometimes resettled her wings.

"Her."

"Her who?"

"Belle's angel. Sometimes I think she moves."

Maddy shuddered. "You're just trying to scare me. Don't."

"I'm not trying to scare you. I know she's made out of granite or something and can't really move. But sometimes she *seems* to. Just a little. Like she's really tired of standing in the exact same position all this time and has to change her wings around a little. And every time I see her do it—or *think* I see her do it—I feel . . ."

"Feel how?"

Rose sighed. "Jittery. Deep down."

She felt change coming. And she didn't want change because she loved her world exactly as it was—when their days cycled through the year the same way over and over: spring calves, summer haying, fall calves, winter stillness—each year repeating the same as the year before. Yet there were always adventures. Like driving. Or moving. Or folding a square of paper so it turned unexpectedly into a dragon or an angel. Or stumbling upon a newly dropped calf curled up in the spring grass.

She sensed Maddy beside her staring at the angel. "Is she moving now?" Maddy asked.

Rose watched for a while. "No." Though before she turned completely away, she might have seen a slight shifting. She told herself she was being silly.

They got back into bed, but Rose was wide awake now.

Maddy fidgeted on her side of the bed. Finally, she turned on her side to face Rose. "You know what I heard?"

"What?"

"I heard my dad tell my mom that your mom is back in town. That he saw her in the Walmart parking lot."

Something in Rose closed like a drawstring being yanked tight. She couldn't breathe. If her mother came back she would ruin things and hurt Ama again.

"Do you remember her?" Maddy asked.

"Not really."

There was one little scrap of memory. Her mother was in the kitchen and Rose did something really bad. She couldn't remember what. But it made Ama so angry that Iris ran off. What Rose remembered like it was ten minutes ago was Ama gathering Rose onto her lap and hugging her until Rose couldn't breathe. She felt Ama's heart bouncing under her shirt and her whole body trembling. "You're my girl," Ama said. Rose clung to Ama, sobbing, so sorry for the bad thing she'd done. Or maybe Ama was sobbing. Myrtle, who was brand-new, was peeing on the floor.

"I saw Iris once," Rose told Maddy. "But I was so young I don't really remember."

"How old were you?"

"About three. Myrtle was a puppy."

She shut her eyes against the too-bright stars. After she'd started to school and heard what kids said, she'd asked Ama if her mother had been wild and a druggie, but the questions made Ama look so sad Rose didn't have the heart to really try to get answers. All Ama said was that Iris had been too young for motherhood.

Dread of Iris's coming back built in Rose until her mind was going around and around with the terrible things that would happen if her mother showed up. Ama might get so mad she had a heart attack. Iris really might be the druggie wild thing kids at school talked about, and Rose would be ashamed. Rose might do something wrong again. Something dangerous. Her mother was dangerous.

Rose caught her breath and made herself exhale slowly. She tried to relax, to stop worrying. She imagined a square piece of paper. She folded it in half, opened it, rotated it, and folded it in half again. She opened it and brought the four corners to the middle and creased the edges. She folded that square in half. She folded on, going somewhere, not sure where.

Gradually, Maddy began to snore and Rose couldn't follow the folds. Her last thought was that Uncle Thomas was probably mistaken.

·· eight ··

ROSE poked through the pile of paper on her desk. Tomorrow, June 20, was Ama's birthday. Maybe it was after midnight and already tomorrow. Ama and Myrtle had been asleep for a long time. Even the June bugs had called it a night. A breeze wafted through the window, ruffling the stack of paper and drying the sweat on Rose's neck.

She found a piece of purple wrapping paper that would be good for making lotus petals. She cut, creased, rolled, and curled, and then she glued the petals together and added gold thread to make the hairy center. Finally, she chose a fancy gold bead from her art stash for the seedpod. And *voilà!* She had a splendid purple lotus.

She rubbed her eyes. She'd already made a rose and a tulip. Ama's birthday cake was going to be square, and Rose wanted a flower for each side. Because of the names in the family— Lotus, Tulip, Iris, Rose—the fourth flower should be an iris, but Ama wouldn't want her birthday cake to remind her. Ama never brought up Iris, and when someone asked about her, Ama answered without really saying anything.

Ama had told Maddy the other day the surprise lily was her favorite flower, and the family party tomorrow was a surprise. So Rose would make a lily instead of an iris.

Folding an origami lily with fancy inner folds had been her demonstration project in 4-H. She had folded so many practice lilies she could do it with her eyes closed—though she was afraid if she shut her eyes she would fall asleep. She dug through the stack to find crisp pink tissue paper, cut an eight-and-a-half-inch square, and began to fold. In no time, she had a beautiful lily Ama would love.

The next morning, after their chores and breakfast, Ama said, "I think I'll work in the garden this morning."

Something in her eyes told Rose the surprise party wasn't really a surprise.

"The potatoes need to be hilled," Ama said. "The tomatoes need to be staked. The whole garden needs weeding. And I'll pick us peas for lunch." She smiled at Rose. "I'll probably be out there all morning."

Rose couldn't help the smile that broke out on her own face. "Okay," she said. "I'll be in here."

Rose had found a splendid cake online—four layers tall, with frothy white icing, decorated with little silver balls called *dragées,* which Aunt Carol had ordered for Rose. The paper flowers around the cake on the pink pedestal platter from one of the Greats would make it even more regal.

88

Rose used two boxes of chocolate cake mix to make the four layers, so the actual cake part was easy. While the pans cooled on racks, she turned to the online frosting recipe.

She mixed sugar, water, syrup, and salt in a pan and brought it to a boil. But she didn't understand what it meant to *boil until the mixture will spin a long thread when a little is dropped from a spoon (hold the spoon high above the saucepan)*. She watched the mixture bubble.

She still had to separate the yolks from three eggs and beat the whites into soft peaks, which she had never done before.

She hadn't expected things to take so long.

The syrup mixture was shrinking in the pan, bubbles breaking with pops and spatters. *Hold the spoon high above the saucepan,* the directions said.

Rose got the stepladder from the garage.

The mixture will spin a long thread when a little is dropped from a spoon.

She scooped a little into the spoon, climbed the ladder, and leaned over the stove. Sweat prickled her face as she tipped a tiny bit of the sticky amber liquid out of the spoon.

She jumped and threw the spoon when suddenly a person was standing right there in the doorway between the kitchen and the dining room. She had spikes of pink and orange hair fanned over a wide black headband and fake eyelashes so long and thick she reminded Rose of a llama. Rose knew who she was. She was tall like Lotus. She had Great-aunt Annie's

89

freckles. She was without a doubt an older version of the pictures of Rose's mother in the albums. Alarm bells went off from somewhere in Rose's memory of her mother. Her knees tried to turn to noodles, but she locked them.

They stared at each other.

Finally, her mother said, "Where's Ma?" She picked up the tissue paper lily on the counter.

"Please put that down." Rose's voice shook.

Iris's face turned red.

"It's Ama's favorite flower," Rose said. "A surprise lily."

Iris blinked, something flashing in her expression before she looked away. Carefully, she put the flower down. "Sorry."

Then she asked why Rose was on a ladder.

"Because." She shouldn't be talking to her mother.

Iris stepped to the stove and peered into the pan. "What are you cooking?"

"Frosting."

"Ma makes frosting with butter and milk and powdered sugar. She doesn't cook it."

"This is special. For her birthday." The words moved tight and breathy through Rose's pinched throat. Why didn't she shut up?

The door between the garage and the kitchen flew open and Ama stood there.

"Happy birthday, Ma."

Surprise, anger, and worry clouded Ama's face. The doorbell rang.

Rose scrambled off the ladder. "I'll get it." She stumbled as she passed her mother.

When she opened the door, Uncle Thomas held a Crock-Pot, Maddy waggled a gift bag, and Aunt Carol clutched a skinny loaf of bread as long as Rose's arms.

"Is something burning?" Aunt Carol asked.

"The frosting," Rose mumbled.

"Frosting is beastly." Aunt Carol said things like *beastly* because she was from England. And she insisted Rose call her *auhnt* instead of *ant* because she was a human, not a bug. When Rose said *auhnt* she felt like she had to lift her chin so high she might step in something. Aunt Carol's hair didn't move. And she always wore lipstick, mascara, and nail polish.

Ama came into the living room looking dazed and awkward. When Iris followed, everybody gawked.

"Happy birthday, Tulip!" Aunt Carol finally said. "We've brought lunch. Hello, Iris." Aunt Carol put down the Crock-Pot and kissed the air beside Iris's cheek. "It's been *such* a long time. Clara's funeral?" She stepped back, studying Iris.

The smile that peeked through the llama mask warmed Iris's face and the alarm bells blared in Rose's head.

Then, acting as if Iris were only slightly unexpected, Aunt Carol motioned. "Come on, girls. Let's put the finishing touches on that birthday cake."

On the way to the kitchen, Rose brushed against Ama and leaned in for a hug. Ama's arm slid around Rose as always, and she gave Rose a squeeze, but there was no heart in it. Rose wanted to kick something. This was Ama's birthday, and Rose had worked hard to make it special. Her mother had picked the worst possible time to show up.

In the kitchen, at least Aunt Carol didn't ask about the ladder, which Rose appreciated. Feeling like her feet were stuck in mud, she folded it and put it in the garage. When she came back, Aunt Carol was pouring the burnt sticky stuff down the drain.

She got butter out of the refrigerator. "Let's just make a nice buttercream frosting, shall we?"

Rose opened her mouth to say that wasn't fancy enough; then she shut it.

As Aunt Carol whipped up frosting she kept saying things like "Goodness! *Four layers?*"

"It's a special occasion," Rose said.

"Now it's *really* special," Maddy said, practically wagging her tail with interest. "With *her* here." Leaning close, she whispered, "I *told* you my dad had seen her."

Rose narrowed her eyes at Maddy. If Rose had known her mother was coming, she would have locked the door to keep Ama from being upset, especially today.

"Bugs could get caught in those lashes," Maddy said, giggling. "But otherwise, you two look just alike."

"We do not!"

Aunt Carol arched her eyebrows at them and asked Rose to please measure the vanilla.

When the frosting was creamy, Rose spread it. Little bits of cake broke off and had to be stuck back on, which took extra frosting. Plus, putting four layers on top of each other without everything leaning was nearly impossible.

"I want to help!" Maddy kept saying, standing about an inch away, with her nose practically *in* the frosting.

Getting every last bit of chocolate cake covered so no brown patches showed called for yet more frosting, which Aunt Carol whipped up.

"And this is absolutely all," Aunt Carol said, "because we're out of confectioners' sugar."

"It's *huge*," Maddy said when the fourth layer was settled on top and spread with the last of the frosting.

Rose decided to skip the little silver balls after Maddy put one in her mouth and said it was hard as a rock and tasted like soap. Rose placed an origami flower on each side of the cake, and Aunt Carol took a picture before Rose carried the cake into the living room. It was so heavy her hands shook.

And there sat her mother, who Rose had actually forgotten about for a few minutes.

When Ama saw the cake, she shook her head. Did that mean she couldn't believe Rose had made it all by herself? That it was too beautiful for words? Or did it mean Ama couldn't think about it right now because Iris was here?

Fighting back tears and about to drop the platter, Rose put it on the sideboard. Then she and Maddy and Aunt Carol set the table for lunch. The day was *nothing* like it was supposed to be. It was supposed to be Ama and Rose. Uncle Thomas and Aunt Carol and Maddy. And Myrtle.

While they were eating, Aunt Carol chattered about their upcoming trip to England. They would stay with her sisters and let Maddy get to know her cousins. Iris was silent, staring at the sideboard full of pretty china from Grandma Clara's day. The rug under the table that had always been there. The lamp in the corner that threw the light up on the ceiling instead of down on the floor. The framed photograph on the wall of Great-great-grandpa Franklin Lovell in overalls leaning on an axe handle, pieces of chopped wood at his feet. And another picture of him with his three brothers as young men standing in front of a wagon piled high with hay. Iris's gaze rested a long time on the pair of framed hands-holding-flowers prints signed by Lotus Lovell.

When Iris was Rose's age, she had sat in this very room at this very table, maybe in that very chair. Had everybody loved each other then? Had her mother been happy?

Rose felt dizzy, as if she'd looked at the smooth surface of the pond and seen things deeper than her own reflection. She felt a sinking feeling, which felt a little like sympathy.

"I like your nails, Iris," Maddy said.

Iris glanced at her glossy black nails with tiny silver stars on each tip. "Thanks," she said with that smile again that warmed her face.

Did Maddy really like them? Black fingernails were nasty. But a memory tugged at Rose of her mother with long silky hair and pink nails. And she'd smelled nice. There was something about that day Rose couldn't remember. Sometimes it almost snuck back, but when she tried to whirl and grab it, it slipped away.

When Iris caught Rose watching her, Rose turned and kept her gaze fixed on Ama. Ama's face was pale.

"Tulip," Uncle Thomas was saying, "remember how Harriet Jane just turned up after Grandpa died? Just out of the blue?"

Ama looked at him, seeming for a second not to know what he was talking about. But then she nodded. "I was at the barn and saw this person coming toward me. I'd never seen her in my life, but I knew who it was." Her cheeks colored and she shot Uncle Thomas a look. "It was my sister."

Uncle Thomas nodded.

What had made Uncle Thomas think of Harriet Jane? Had he also noticed Iris staring at the bouquet prints? Or was it just Iris's turning up out of the blue the way Harriet Jane had done?

"I was fifteen then," Uncle Thomas said. "And mightily impressed. The Mystery Aunt returned. And remember how it cheered us up? We thought the farm was lost and we were going to have to find other vocations." He smiled. "Which I did anyway, but then I was convinced I wanted to farm. And like a fairy godmother, Harriet Jane swished into the bank and paid off the debt. Remember how happy Grandma Clara was?"

Ama nodded, smiling for the first time.

"Of course, she was grieving Grandpa's death," Uncle Thomas said. "But she had her oldest child back, and the farm was safe."

"And then she died," Ama said quietly.

Rose knew Ama meant Harriet Jane had died. Grandma Clara had lived a long time after that.

"But not for a while," Uncle Thomas said. "Remember how she'd speak Italian for us? And she showed us pictures of that little mountain town in Tuscany where she lived? Of her apartment above the linen shop on the town square. And her sculptures. And her friends."

Ama nodded. "It was like she'd been on a different planet. All those grape and olive vineyards on those hillsides. The Biblical skies."

They were quiet for a while. Forks tapped plates and Rose's food tasted like cardboard. Normally, she loved stories about the old days and the Greats, but today, with her mother here, even those felt dangerous.

A while later, when Aunt Carol served the cake, Rose watched Ama take a bite.

"Delicious," Uncle Thomas pronounced. "Did you make this, Rose?"

"Yes."

Ama smiled, but she put down her fork. She didn't like the cake.

Rose took a bite. It tasted very ordinary. Not special at all. The cake would have tasted excellent if her mother hadn't showed up.

Aunt Carol was asking Iris about her job at the salon like Iris was her favorite niece. And Maddy was looking admiringly at Iris's dangly earrings. Maddy was probably about to say she loved them.

"I don't think it's right to show up after years and years and expect people to just pass the potatoes," Rose blurted, interrupting Aunt Carol.

Ama's eyes flicked to Rose and she started to say something.

"What potatoes?" Maddy said.

"Honey, I think Rose meant . . . ," Aunt Carol began.

"May I be excused?" Rose didn't wait for an answer.

She'd hardly eaten, but she felt like her lunch might come up. She ran outside and threw herself into the porch swing. Myrtle, who could open the screen door, came out and sat at her feet until Rose patted the space beside her and Myrtle leapt into the swing and onto Rose's lap.

When Maddy came out, she sat down and they rocked back and forth. After a while, Maddy said quietly, "Is she anything like you expected?"

Rose shook her head.

"Oh well," Maddy said. "I bought a French manicure kit with babysitting money. Let's do our nails."

She jumped out of the swing and ran to the car to get the manicure kit.

"Come on," she said. "Let's go to your room."

As they went up the stairs, voices were still coming from the dining room. But in Rose's room, Iris was sitting on Rose's bed.

"I've not been up here in years," she said. "This was my bed." She traced the delicate metal headboard of birds and flowers with her fingers. "You painted it white."

"No, I didn't. It's always been white."

"It was green when it was mine." Iris scratched off a flake of paint with one of her shiny black nails. "See? Green underneath."

Rose scowled. She hadn't given Iris permission to come in and sit on her bed and scratch off paint. "Well, I didn't paint it."

"I guess Ma did. It's pretty this way."

Before she turned to look out the window, she smiled at Rose as if maybe they could be friends. But Iris was a grown-up and Rose was a kid. And Iris was her mother, even though Rose could never think of her like that. And Rose couldn't think of Iris as someone like Aunt Carol because she just couldn't, because Iris was her mother. But not really.

The sun, which had been behind clouds, suddenly slid out and the room brightened. The shadow boxes caught the light.

Iris crossed the room to look. "Did you make these?" She sounded truly interested.

"Yes."

Iris studied the shadow boxes. "They're good." She pointed to the one in the middle. "That's Ma. And you. And the dog. And the cows. You got the sky just right," she said. "When I was growing up here, I loved the sky. The sky in Kentucky is nothing like this one. Actually, the sky in town is nothing like this one."

"And look at these," Maddy said, going to Rose's bulletin board. "Blue ribbon, blue ribbon, blue ribbon."

Iris looked.

Then her eyes riveted on the bottom shelf of the glass-fronted bookcase. "Those are my dolls." She sounded surprised. "Ma kept them." She went to the bookcase and sat cross-legged on the floor. She raised the glass door and slid it back. She picked the dolls up, one by one, turning them, running her fingers over them. Rose couldn't see Iris's face.

Maddy was looking at Rose as if to say *This is pretty weird*, and Rose felt embarrassed. She turned and left the room, motioning to Maddy to follow her.

They went downstairs. "We can do the manicures on the porch," Rose said. She still felt mad at Iris for turning up and ruining Ama's surprise party. And she'd be glad when her mother was gone. But the way Iris held and touched the dolls was sad.

"Why do you think she's come back after all this time?" Maddy asked as she spread out her manicure stuff on the porch floor. "Do you suppose she's come for you?"

Rose rolled her eyes and said, *"No,"* like it was the stupidest idea in the world. "Does she look like she could be my mother? She's so young. Besides, Ama adopted me years ago."

"You're adopted?" Maddy looked astonished.

"Well, yeah. Didn't you know that?"

Maddy shook her head. "I thought Aunt Tulip was just your grandmother."

"She is. My grandmother who legally adopted me when I was four years old."

Maddy sighed. "My life is so boring."

Maddy gave Rose a French manicure; then she wanted Rose to give her one. Myrtle came out to see what they were doing but didn't like the smell and went back inside. Rose wondered if Iris was still upstairs. She wondered what Ama was doing.

After a while, Aunt Carol came to the door to check on them.

"Where's Ama?" Rose asked.

"Closed up in her office with Iris," Aunt Carol said.

Rose had an uneasy feeling in her stomach.

Aunt Carol went away, and Rose and Maddy blew on Maddy's nails to dry them faster. They were gingerly touching them to test when Iris came through the door. She went around them where they sat on the steps without saying anything. Rose glanced at her, but she couldn't see Iris's face. She got in her car and drove off. It was strange that she left without a goodbye.

Soon Uncle Thomas came to the door and said it was almost

time to go. Ama gave them a carton of fresh eggs and a bundle of rhubarb to take home, and then it was just Rose and Ama again.

In the dining room, the cake, too tall to fit in the cake keeper, sat on the sideboard. They'd never be able to eat all of it. And there was way too much frosting. And nobody had mentioned the flowers Rose had stayed up half the night making.

The sun had gone away again, and everything—even Ama—looked the way Rose felt. Flat and listless.

"I need to trim your bangs," Ama said, brushing Rose's hair out of her eyes. "But does a nap sound good right now?"

Rose nodded. Sometimes on Sunday afternoon they all got into Ama's king-sized bed and napped the rest of the day away. Maybe they could sleep off her mother's visit. They would wake up and it would be as if Iris had never been there. And Rose hoped she never came back.

Ama folded her pillow double as always, but her book lay unopened beside her. Rose forgot to kick off her shoes as she lay down. And instead of curling up in a cozy ball at the foot of the bed, Myrtle lay with her head on her paws watching them.

"What did my mom want?" Rose asked, kicking off her shoes and turning to face Ama.

"Just money," Ama said. "She needs a little help right now, and I'm able to give it." Ama took a deep breath and let it out slowly. "So I did. End of story, okay?"

"Okay," Rose said, hoping it was true.

Ama lay back against her pillow and picked up her book.

Rose opened her book. Myrtle still didn't curl into a ball.

"I guess she lives around here now?" Rose said.

"Um," Ama said. "She has an apartment in town. And you heard about her job at a salon."

"Is she going to keep turning up?" That sounded meaner than Rose intended.

"I doubt it," Ama said.

Rose needed a definite no. She loved the wonderful, comfortable sameness of her and Ama's life. She didn't like change unless it was her idea.

She glanced at Ama. Ama's eyes were on her book, but she didn't look relaxed. Usually during Sunday afternoon naps, everybody drooled and snored and woke up three hours later feeling stupid but happy. But Rose was as stiff as a dead bird. Myrtle's eyes flicked from one to the other. This was the worst Sunday afternoon nap ever.

Finally, Ama turned to her other side and put down her novel. Rose looked at Ama's thick gray-blond hair, the rim of her ear just peeking out, her broad shoulders, the freckles on the backs of her arm. Ama was Rose's rock and her pillow.

She couldn't tell if Ama had really fallen asleep or was playing possum. Myrtle still watched them with bright eyes.

Eventually Rose fell into a worn-out doze and twitched with strange, sudden dreams.

In the late afternoon, she got up, trying to be quiet because

Ama was still sleeping. She slipped out of the house and headed for the barn. It was very still, as if the whole world were taking a Sunday nap.

She heard the back door and turned, seeing Ama and Myrtle coming out.

As they walked along the lane, Ama pulled Rose to her side and kissed her head. "Everything will be fine. Let's not worry."

Ama stayed with Rose while she made Peanutbutter's bottle and fed the calf.

Giving Peanutbutter her full attention so she didn't have to look at Ama, she asked, "What was my mother like when she was my age?"

When Ama didn't answer, Rose said, "Did you ever walk over to the barn with her to feed a calf, like we're doing now?"

"Oh, I'm sure I did," Ama said almost as if it were a silly question.

Rose had felt a pang of envy. She didn't like sharing Ama, even if it was a long time ago.

Ama made an odd noise. "Truthfully, I'm not sure I did. Everything was different then. But if I didn't, her dad did."

"So Grandpa was still here when Iris was my age?"

"Oh yes. They both left about the same time."

Ama said it so breezily Rose felt how much it had hurt. Why would anyone leave Ama? Why would anyone leave this wonderful place?

"I'll never leave," Rose said.

Ama kissed her on top of the head.

While Rose finished the chores with Peanutbutter, Ama fed the steers that were penned up ready to go to the sale barn.

When she came back, Rose was just finishing her record-keeping.

"I think you should try leading Peanutbutter around the barnyard," Ama said.

"Really?" Rose had been wanting to try it, but Peanutbutter weighed a lot more than her and was still pretty rowdy.

"Really. You've been faithful about working with the rope and halter. Let's see how she does outside the stall. Just keep the rope short." Ama showed her how to hold it.

Excitement shook Rose's hands as she untied Peanutbutter. She held the rope the way Ama said. Ama opened the gate.

Rose's heart raced as she expected Peanutbutter to dart outside, but Peanutbutter just stood there.

"Walk forward," Ama said, "and see what she does."

Peanutbutter dug in her feet and pulled back. Rose tugged. Peanutbutter tugged. Ama went behind Peanutbutter and touched her hindquarters and the calf ambled forward.

"Keep her close," Ama said softly, "and just keep walking."

Every time Peanutbutter balked, Ama touched her rear end. And after a while, Peanutbutter got the hang of it. Rose led her calf around the barnyard feeling so proud she could practically touch the stars.

"I think you've got a good calf there," Ama said.

"She's a fine little heifer," Rose said, smiling inside.

When she'd done all her evening tasks, she wrote in the record book *Led Peanutbutter around the barnyard for the first time!*

By the time they left the barn, the sky was a deep, dark purple and whippoorwills were calling.

They stopped and looked at the stars, which were fully out. When Rose was little she'd believed the sky over their farm was theirs alone. She'd called it *our sky.*

She found the Little Dipper in the north sky and then the polestar. She'd learned in science it was the only star that stayed put as the other constellations seemed to rotate around it, but it was really the earth rotating around the sun.

"Do you like being on a moving planet?" she asked Ama. "I don't really."

Ama drew Rose to her. "I remember looking at the stars with my dad," she said. "We talked about that too. I haven't thought about it in years."

"What was your dad like?"

"When I was your age, I adored him. He was a stubborn man. But I knew him later in life when he'd mellowed."

As they passed the chicken pen, Ama used a flashlight to search out the two Wyandottes, which had gone to sleep in the grass. She put them in the chicken house, then closed the door.

#

Rose had brushed Ama's hair, and now Ama was brushing Rose's hair. Tonight, for some reason, tears began to roll down

Rose's cheeks. She had been thinking of the angel in the cemetery and how she seemed to shift her wings as if getting ready for something. It was silly. The angel didn't really do that. But that was what Rose was thinking about when the tears started.

··nine··

ROSE didn't know what pulled her from the dream that slipped away forgotten. The wind was blowing like a storm was coming. Maybe thunder had woken her.

She got out of bed and went to the west window. A swell of lightning showed a car in the drive. She crossed the hall to the listening post she and Maddy had discovered a few summers ago when they were playing hide-and-seek. That day, Maddy had been hiding and accidentally kicked away a piece of baseboard, exposing a hole in the wall. When Rose put her hand inside because Maddy dared her—even though a person never knew what was in a dark hole—she felt a pipe that ran down and up. And then Ama said *I'm calling to make an appointment* as clearly as if she were under the desk with them. Rose and Maddy heard the opening and closing of the refrigerator. And Myrtle crunching her dog food.

Rose lay on her stomach and pulled away the baseboard.

"What's so important it couldn't wait until morning?" Ama asked, her voice tired.

"I have to tell you something." It was Iris's voice.

She was back already. Stress knotted Rose's stomach.

"You have to tell me in the middle of the night?" Ama asked.

"It's important," Iris said.

Rose heard rustling and then Ama said, "So tell me."

"I'm afraid to. You make it so hard to talk to you about anything," Iris said. "You've always been that way."

Thunder was rumbling now and Rose had to strain to hear.

"I come to tell you something, to confide in you, and you make it so hard. I would have told you earlier if you'd been more open. If you'd seemed to care about me." There was a long silence, then Iris said, "Are you still mad about Rose?"

Rose jumped when Ama cried out. She'd never heard Ama make such a sound.

"Am I still mad?" Ama sounded as if she could blow up the house. Or the world. "You say that like you accidentally tracked in mud. You dumped Rose on me!"

Puppies were dumped. Kittens were dumped. Trash was dumped. Rose put her arms over her head as Ama threw words like rocks. They hurt so much.

"I didn't have a car seat. Or a crib. Or baby clothes. I didn't have diapers or formula except for what was in her bag. I didn't have help. I had so many things I had to take care of. And I was all by myself. My mom was dying and your dad had left me."

"I know, Ma."

"Shut up. You don't have any idea. I used to stand in the

shower until the water ran cold so I couldn't hear Rose's screams."

Rose's very breath went out of her. Ama had let her cry? Hadn't come to pick her up and cuddle her? Hadn't kissed her and rocked her? That couldn't be true.

"Newborns have to be fed constantly," Ama said. "Did you know that?"

Silence.

"Did you know that?" Ama said.

"Yes, Ma."

"Around the clock. Every day. Day after day."

Iris didn't say anything.

Tears washed Rose's face. She'd been a bad baby.

"I was so tired after a few weeks I couldn't go on. I called social services to come and get her."

Rose felt like she'd been blown up in an explosion. Her head rang. Ama's words rained down. Rose had almost been given away. By *Ama*. Ama wasn't who Rose thought she was. Rose herself wasn't who she thought she was. She was just some screaming baby in a blanket to be handed to strangers.

She stumbled to her feet as tears scalded her face. She could never face Ama again.

In her room, she turned on a light and yanked on yesterday's clothes. Trying to keep the tears wiped away, she found her backpack and crammed in a few clothes, paper and scissors, toothbrush and hairbrush. She rushed down the stairs.

The sound of her opening and closing the front door was drowned out by rain lashing the windows. Lightning billowed as she ran for the shelter of Iris's car. Hunkering in the back, she sobbed.

Before long, Iris yanked open the car door and got behind the wheel. Rose balled up on the floor and choked back her tears. She was running away forever.

Iris barreled along the country roads, bouncing through potholes. Rose was icy. She couldn't quit shaking. Her teeth were chattering. She was never going back. Myrtle would wonder what had happened to her. So would Peanutbutter. Rose wished she'd packed her shadow boxes. She felt her sobs but couldn't hear them because of the rain pounding the car.

Finally, Iris reached the highway and turned right. They were heading toward town. Rose's mind thrashed. She didn't know what to do, where to go, but the minute the car stopped, she'd jump out and run into the darkness and none of them would ever see her again. Nobody wanted her and she didn't want them.

On the highway, Iris picked up speed and drove fast even though rain was pouring down. She turned on music so loud Rose felt like she was inside a drum. She was getting carsick, especially when Iris drove through low places and water surged against the bottom of the car.

Finally, the car bumped over the railroad tracks east of town. In a few blocks Iris would stop at the stop sign and Rose would make her move.

When the car slowed, Rose uncurled and sat up. Iris's scream sliced through the music and Rose was pitched suddenly forward and then back, banging her head, seeing stars and hearing crashing sounds.

Iris cried, "You made me rear-end that guy!"

She threw the car in reverse, stomped the brakes, and speeded away. Rose peered out the back window. An angry man stood in the rain.

"What are you doing back there?" Iris screeched.

"I'm sorry! Pull over and let me out."

Iris turned off the music. "I'm lucky the car still runs! Why are you in here?" Her voice was high.

"Just let me out."

"I don't think so," Iris said, and Rose heard the sound of the doors locking.

Rose tried to open the door. "I mean it. Let me out!"

Iris kept driving, muttering.

Finally, she parked behind an apartment building. She brought out her phone. "I'm calling Ma."

"No!" Rose snatched the phone and sat on it.

"What's gotten into you? You're her little calf, mooning around like you can't bear to leave her side for a second."

Rose crossed her arms and stared into space.

After a while, Iris said, "You were listening, weren't you?"

Rose tried to look puzzled.

"Don't think you're the first person to discover that hole

behind the baseboard. That was my bedroom for fifteen years. So now I know what you're in such a snit about."

They sat in silence. Iris couldn't possibly know anything about how Rose felt.

Finally, Iris said, "May I please have my phone?"

"Not if you're going to call her." Rose was clammy in her soaked clothes. Her head felt like it was stuffed with cotton balls and might split open any second.

"Look. I'll let Ma know you're with me. You can stay here until morning and get calmed down. How's that?"

The minute Iris went to sleep, Rose would run. She could take care of herself. She didn't need Ama. She didn't need anybody. "No double-crossing?"

Iris sounded tired. "No. I'm just exhausted and want to go to bed."

Rose handed over the phone.

Iris unlocked the car doors and gave Rose a key. "Go on up. Second floor. Apartment 212. Be quiet and don't wake anybody. I'll tell Ma you're okay, then I'll be up."

Rose hoisted her backpack over her shoulder. The rain had tapered to a sprinkle, and it stopped by the time she got to the door.

Her shoes squished as she walked down the stuffy hall with a million doors. She had never been inside an apartment building before. So many people crammed together felt creepy. She let herself into apartment 212, which smelled even worse than the hall.

The room was dimly lit by a silent television. A lumpy person snored on the floor. There was a big window with the curtain closed, but the parking lot lights still turned the room a dingy yellow. Two chairs and a table were heaped with boxes. Rose leaned her backpack against the wall.

Did the lumpy person on the floor live here?

When Iris tapped on the door, Rose let her in.

Iris put her finger to her lips, laid her car keys on the kitchen counter, and motioned to Rose to follow. As they walked down a short hall, Rose saw a bathroom on the left lit by a night-light. A room across the hall had the door open a crack. When they reached the room at the end, Iris flipped on a light.

Rose squinted in the sudden brightness as bugs disappeared in an instant among the stuff spilling out of boxes. Piles of clothes and dirty dishes were on the floor by one side of the bare mattress. The room smelled musty.

"This is just for one night," Iris whispered. "You take that side." She pointed to the side where the mess wasn't. She tossed Rose a shirt from one of the piles. "Here. You can sleep in this."

"No thanks," Rose said.

Iris shrugged. "Suit yourself."

Rose put her head on a pillow that was too bouncy. Her wet clothes clung to her.

Down the hall, Iris talked quietly to someone; then the door to the apartment opened and closed.

This was like another planet a hundred earth years from

home. Everything that raced through Rose's mind was something she couldn't bear to think about. Iris turned off the light and lay down beside her. A car honked over and over, making Rose's heart race. Voices from the hallway came through the wall. She was afraid the people could just push through the thin wall if they wanted to and step right into the room.

When Iris's phone vibrated she answered sleepily.

Rose heard Ama's voice.

"Ma wants to talk to you," Iris said.

Rose's throat burned. "No," she whispered.

"She's okay, Ma. She's just upset."

Rose put her hands over her ears so she couldn't hear Ama's voice. Tears scalded her cheeks.

Iris got off the phone and turned away, pulling the sheet around her.

After a while, Rose could tell Iris was asleep.

Rose rehearsed her moves. Get up, grab the backpack, slip out of the apartment, rush down the hall, run across the parking lot, disappear into the shadows.

She ordered herself to get up and get going, but she lay as stiff and unmoving as a pencil.

Tears started again. She was trying to muffle her sobs when something moved along her side of the mattress and stopped. Rose gasped. Eyes shone in the darkness. Rose's heart nearly jumped out of her chest.

She made out a silhouette of curls; then a small hand touched

Rose's side, right in the ticklish part of her ribs. Rose tried not to jump.

The hand patted over Rose's bare arm, across her shoulder. When it touched Rose's face, Rose smelled peanut butter. The baby crawled onto Rose's body. It was unbelievably soft as Rose steadied it.

The small head came close, breath tickling Rose's face.

They stayed nose to nose until the baby made kind of a nest out of Rose, tucking its head under Rose's chin. Rose's arms crossed over it.

·· ten ··

*L*OUD knocking woke Rose into a room bright with sun. Her eyes were swollen slits. She tried to remember where she was. She rolled over and saw a small head with a froth of dark curls.

The knocking was still going on. Rose sat up as Iris scrambled out of bed. As Iris left the room, she glanced back at Rose.

Rose panicked, knowing it was Ama knocking on the apartment door. The window air conditioner sent a river of cold over her as she rushed to wedge a chair under the doorknob. She couldn't face her grandmother.

Soon, there was a tap on the bedroom door. "Rose? Can I come in? Please?"

Tears seeped out of Rose's sore eyes at the sound of Ama's voice. She longed to run into Ama's arms, but Ama had broken her heart.

"Sweetheart, let me in."

The door opened a crack before the chair stopped it. Rose froze behind the door, out of sight.

"Oh, Rose. Please. I need to explain."

The baby on the bed, naked except for a diaper, sat up and began to jabber.

Ama gasped.

As the baby babbled, she waved her hands and arms. Her delicate winglike brows came together in a scowl. Rose couldn't take her eyes off her.

She felt Ama on the other side of the door staring too. Then Ama said, "Oh no." She sounded like she'd come across a two-headed calf in the pasture.

Ama went away from the door and she and Iris began to argue about the baby and how Iris lived, their voices rising.

The baby squirmed off the mattress and stumbled across the room, tripping over stuff. She stopped in front of Rose. Sweaty curls matted one cheek.

Rose touched the child's dimpled hand. The child studied Rose's finger, pale against her skin, then Rose's face.

"What's your name?" Rose said quietly, under the sound of the shouting.

The child looked away as if she were thinking. "Illy," she decided.

"Lily?" Ama's favorite flower. Why had Iris named her that? Rose touched her chest. "I'm Rose."

Lily pressed her face to the crack in the door, then looked at Rose with worry as if to say *What's going on out there?*

Rose shook her head. She didn't want to hear what Ama and

Iris were saying to each other, but she couldn't help it. Gently, she put her hands over Lily's ears.

Ama was accusing Iris of not taking charge of her life. Of not being *responsible*! Of barely managing day to day. And now of bringing *another child* into the world. A child she could no more take care of than the man in the moon. Did Iris expect Ama to raise *that* child too? Well, *she wasn't going to!* Hearing Ama carry on like that broke Rose's heart all over again. And Iris was yelling that she had tried to tell Ama about Lily, but Ama wouldn't listen. And, of course, Ama didn't understand that sometimes you didn't have perfect control of your life. Things just happened! And Iris was sorry she wasn't perfect, but neither was Ama.

"All I need, Ma, is a little help and understanding," Iris said.

"You need way more than a little help and understanding. You need to grow up and take responsibility for your behavior!"

Rose's head pounded.

Then Ama was outside the bedroom door again. "Rose Elizabeth Lovell, you open that door right now and let me in."

Rose shrank back. Ama had never talked to her that way.

When Lily cowered beside Rose, Rose's arm went around her.

"Rose!" Ama's voice boomed.

Iris was crying. "Please, Ma. You'll get me kicked out."

"Rose!" Ama said again, but not as loudly. "Let me in! You're going home with me right now." Ama pushed against the door and the chair shifted, but it stayed wedged under the doorknob.

Wide-eyed and with her lip quivering, Lily looked up at Rose.

Even if Rose wanted to see Ama, which she didn't, she couldn't leave Lily. When you found an abandoned calf in the pasture, you took care of it. And Rose had found a baby sister.

Ama's voice dropped to a whisper. "Rose, please, please, please. This is no place for you."

"Lily's really scared," Rose said.

"Lily?"

"The baby. Her name is Lily."

Rose could hear Ama breathing.

"Can we keep her?" Rose asked. "Just for a while?"

"No, we cannot," Ama said.

"Then I'm staying." Rose couldn't believe she'd said that. Her heart was still broken, but she didn't want to stay here in this dark, messy place. She wanted to go home.

When Ama started to cry, Rose's hand went to the chair. She'd heard Ama cry only once before, and she couldn't bear it. But Lily was looking at her with those dark eyes that said *I don't have a good mama. Please don't leave me.*

After a while, Ama moved away from the door.

Shortly, Iris said, "Ma's gone. You can let me in."

Her whole body trembling, Rose moved the chair.

Iris rushed in. "That went well," she said in a tone that

meant just the opposite. "I can't believe you didn't go with her." She gathered up clothes and disappeared into the bathroom. The shower went on.

Rose knelt in front of Lily. "Don't worry," she said, "everything will be okay." She didn't understand how that could possibly be true, but she needed to sound encouraging.

Lily babbled something, then tugged at the sides of her diaper until it dropped to the floor. She walked around naked, pawing through boxes in the messiest room Rose had ever seen.

Rose found her backpack and dug through it for shorts and a T-shirt. She felt like Lily, rummaging through stuff, and it made her so sad she could hardly move. How could she not be going home with Ama? To Myrtle and fresh air and the wonder of her new room?

She took her clothes into Iris's bedroom and changed. Lily had wriggled into one of Iris's sparkly tops. She put her hands on her potbelly and smiled at Rose. The sequined shirt dragged on the floor as she stumbled down the hallway.

Rose followed. As she passed the room where the door had been partly shut last night, she stopped and stared. It was another shamble of boxes and piles. The only furniture was a stained, bare twin-sized mattress on the floor. Rose cringed at the idea of Lily sleeping on that.

In the living room, Lily plopped down in front of the silent TV.

Rose's stomach rumbled.

The refrigerator was full of diet soft drinks and a few cartons of takeout. Rose peered at the green mold inside one. Inside another was a half-eaten cheeseburger with pickles sticking out from under the bun. Rose loathed pickles. An empty milk carton lay on its side. It had dripped onto the shelf below and left a dried, yellow mess. The refrigerator smelled nasty. Rose shut the door and opened the cupboards.

They were empty.

The cupboards at home overflowed with interesting old stuff left by the Greats, plus Ama and Rose's bowls and pots and pans and the everyday plates with blue flowers. Rose shoved those things to the back of her mind.

She explored the pile on the table. An empty cereal box. Moldy bread. Three kinds of chips, all open. A magazine. A little powdered-sugar-covered donut sliding around in the box. Scotch tape. Scorched hot pads. Parts for a blender. Orange flip-flops. A sticky saucepan. A black patent leather purse with a chain strap.

Why did Iris live like this? Rose had never seen such a thing.

Lily pushed a chair to the kitchen counter, clambered onto it, and tripped on the sparkly shirt. As she stumbled, Rose caught her.

"You're standing on your fancy thing," Rose said. "Lift your feet."

Lily looked at Rose. She pointed. "Dat."

Iris rushed into the kitchen and scooped Lily up. She laid her down on the floor and put a diaper on her in a blink, and Lily scrambled back onto the chair.

"Dat," she said again, pointing harder.

"This?" Rose asked, touching the box of cereal.

Lily scowled. "Dat!" She jabbed her finger.

"What does she want?" Rose asked Iris.

"This?" Iris asked, touching a jar of peanut butter.

Lily beamed and clutched it between both hands after Iris slid it within reach. Lily held the peanut butter out to Rose.

"No, thank you."

Lily scowled and jabbered something.

"What does she want?" Rose asked.

Iris opened the peanut butter jar and went back to her phone.

Lily looked at Rose as if she were stupid. She dipped her hand in the jar and brought up a wad of peanut butter. She opened and closed her fingers; then she began to lick them.

"Yuck," Rose said. "Is that okay?" she asked Iris, who was glaring at her phone.

Iris glanced at Lily and shrugged, then returned to her phone. "These people are crazy. They want me at work half an hour ago. One of the other stylists called in sick."

Iris twisted open a soft drink and looked at Rose. "I can't believe you didn't go with Ma, but since you didn't, do you want a babysitting gig?"

She would be left *alone* with Lily? She didn't know anything about babies.

"The girl who was here last night is as dependable as a squirrel. I can't afford to pay you much, but you'd have food and a place to stay. You could share Lily's room." Iris sounded desperate.

Lily was sitting in front of the TV. The way she licked at the peanut butter made Rose think of Myrtle. Rose shoved the thought away.

This was the closest she'd ever been to a real baby. "I know the Heimlich maneuver," she said.

Iris looked puzzled.

"But not CPR."

Iris's phone vibrated. She stared at the screen for a minute. Then she said, "Will you babysit just for now, at least? I gotta get to work. I can't lose this gig."

"Okay. I guess."

In a couple of minutes, Iris flew past, wearing her llama look again with all the eyelashes. She grabbed her car keys from the counter.

"Here's the door key." She laid it on the counter. "You'll need to buy milk. We're out." She dug in her purse again. "All I've got is a twenty. Don't waste it." She put the bill by the key. "See you later." And she was gone.

Rose stared at the door. That was all?

Maddy had told Rose the proper procedures of babysitting. The parent was supposed to leave a paper with names and telephone numbers. And a time to expect the parent back. And a list of the child's allergies, if any, along with favorite activities and what snack foods could be eaten. Her mother didn't know much about parenting.

Lily was watching her. Lily's face and hands were coated with peanut butter. Rose had an image of an enthusiastic Myrtle leaping on Lily and licking her clean. Tears sprang to Rose's eyes.

She swallowed. "Maybe we should clean your hands and face, Lily."

Lily looked at Rose, but without much interest.

"Come to the sink and let me wash you."

Lily didn't budge.

Rose moved the kitchen chair so it was in front of the sink. "Will you get on the chair so I can wash your hands under the faucet?"

Lily shook her head.

What should Rose do now? She could help move cows from one pasture to another, but she couldn't move a baby. She wished Ama were here to show her how. Or Myrtle. Myrtle would love Lily.

She picked up the peanut butter jar and screwed the lid back on. It was sticky all over. She turned on the faucet. "You want to help me wash dishes?"

Lily's head swiveled.

"Come on." Rose motioned and Lily trotted to the sink.

She lifted Lily onto the chair and soaped her own and Lily's hands and they rubbed and rinsed the peanut butter jar until it was clean. Rose tore off a paper towel and gave it to Lily. "Can you dry it?"

Lily bent over her job.

Rose dampened a paper towel. "Let's clean your face."

Lily turned her face toward Rose.

Rose had never washed another person. The way Lily's soft skin moved was weird. Her eyelids were as thin as flower petals. Rose was afraid of rubbing too hard, but the peanut butter left a film. She cupped Lily's head. Lily was patient while Rose scrubbed.

Finally, Lily's face was clean and shining.

"Thank you," Rose said, her heart pounding as if she'd passed a Brave Girl dare.

"Tank ou," Lily said.

Lily's face and hands were clean, but she smelled. Maybe Rose should wash her all over.

"Would you like to take a bath?" Rose asked.

Lily waddled into the bathroom, her sequined train flowing behind. She climbed into the tub and stoppered the drain.

Rose stripped the sparkly blouse off Lily and turned on the water. There were bubble bath, shampoo, soap, and a frog on the ledge. As Rose poured in bubble bath, the bathroom began to smell like strawberries.

Lily got into the tub and sat down. She looked a little worried as the water continued to rise. When it got to her shoulders, she babbled something.

"I don't understand," Rose said.

Lily grabbed Rose's wrist and tugged.

"You want me to get in?"

Lily beamed.

There was room. Rose and Maddy used to take baths together before Maddy got all modest.

When they were in the tub facing each other, Lily said, "Ose."

Rose wished she could understand.

"Ily," Lily said, patting her own head. She pointed. "Ose."

"Lily and Rose!" Rose felt suddenly, strangely, warm and happy. She splashed her sister. "Lily!"

"Ose!" Lily cried, splashing back.

# #

Lily was like a calf or a puppy, only much prettier and softer. Rose covered Lily's head with a towel and rubbed, trying to be gentle.

"Ose," Lily said as the towel came away, as if she were delighted to see Rose still there.

Rose put the towel over Lily's head again, then lifted it away.

"Ose!" Lily said, bouncing.

They went across the hall to Lily's room.

"Where are your clean clothes?"

Lily looked around and picked up a checked dish towel and held it out to Rose.

Rose shook her head. "Don't worry. We'll find them."

Rose explored the floor of the small room. Ragged, stained towels, three boxes of Kleenex, a plastic bucket, a box of diapers.

"Let's put one of these on you," Rose said, taking out a diaper.

Lily lay down on the floor and was patient as Rose figured out the fastenings, which worked a lot like her baby dolls' diapers.

Rose helped Lily to her feet.

"Now let's find your clothes," Rose said, going back to rummaging through the mess. How could Iris live this way?

Rose found a gold-painted basket with a dead bug caught in a crack, a bottle of pills that could be dangerous to Lily, a Cardinals hoodie, a broken elephant piñata, a pillow shaped like a football, lots of grown-up clothes, and a little red sandal.

"Is this yours?" Rose asked.

Lily beamed and snatched it. "Soos! Illy soos!"

"Where's the other one?"

Lily toddled into Iris's room. In the same place where she'd dropped her diaper this morning, she got on her knees and pawed through things. An image of Myrtle enthusiastically digging for a mole flashed in Rose's mind and blinded her with homesickness.

When Lily found the other sandal, she put it on, pressing the Velcro.

"Wrong foot," Rose said, kneeling and beginning to take off the sandal.

Lily pushed Rose's hands away and put on the other sandal.

"That's not going to be comfortable," Rose said when Lily stood.

Lily scowled and jabbered.

"Okay, okay. Let's find the rest of your clothes. Then we'll go buy milk."

Rose found kids' clothes in a box in Iris's room, but some things looked too big, and some were tight when she tried to put them on Lily. Some smelled sour or had stains. Lily was getting impatient, so when Rose came across a red sundress that tied over the shoulders, even though it was a little large, she dropped it over Lily's head and said, "There! Pretty!"

Lily tried to look down at herself. "Pitty?"

Rose led her into the bathroom and lifted her up. Lily looked at herself in the mirror over the sink. She looked at Rose.

"Illy! Ose!"

Rose put her sister down. She was heavy. But she was nice.

#

The fresh, breezy day was like heaven after the awful apartment. Rose looked around. There was a row of garages and dumpsters, with another apartment building behind them. Across the street, a gas station and a car wash. An intersection.

Across the intersection, a laundromat. And next door, a brick church.

Rose had no idea where to buy milk.

In the parking lot, a white-haired man sat in a car with the window down. Rose didn't see anyone else to ask.

"Excuse me," she said, holding Lily's hand as she went to the window. "I don't live around here. Where could I buy milk?"

The man looked at Lily. "Lily, who's this girl you're babysitting today?"

Lily hung her head, but she smiled at the man and swung Rose's hand back and forth.

The man told Rose, "You have better manners than the girl who's been staying with Lily while her mama's at work."

"Thank you," Rose said.

"To get your milk, there's a Hank and Bank's five or six blocks that way," he said, pointing through the intersection.

That was a long way for Lily to walk.

"I'd drive you, but my daughter says I'm too old and addled. But I like to sit in the car."

Rose nodded. "Thanks for the directions."

"You take good care of that girl, Lily," the man called as they walked away.

Lily turned and waved at him.

Lily walked slowly, holding on to Rose's hand, looking up at things. They'd gone only two blocks when she said, "Owie." She lifted her foot to show Rose.

"What's wrong?"

"Owie," Lily said, shifting from one foot to the next.

Lily had red patches on her feet and Rose's stomach was growling and pinching. She sat on the bench in front of a tattoo parlor and lifted Lily up beside her.

Lily's legs stuck out, showing her sore-looking feet. A strange feeling washed over Rose. With Lily, Rose was a grown-up. She should have made Lily put her shoes on right.

She unfastened the sandals and slid them off. "Better?"

Lily shook her head.

There was no way Rose and Lily could walk to the Hank and Bank's and all the way back to the apartment carrying milk. Lily's regular babysitter must have a car.

A McDonald's was across the street in the next block. Iris had said not to waste money, but they needed food and milk.

"Can you wiggle your toes?" she asked Lily.

Lily looked at her.

Rose kicked off her own shoes and stuck out her feet. "Look. Wiggle your toes."

Lily stared at her toes.

Maybe babies couldn't wiggle their toes. Maddy had probably learned about things like that in her babysitting class. Rose would give anything if Maddy could help her babysit. It would be fun with Maddy. And they could take turns carrying Lily.

She dreaded going back to the dark, messy apartment.

Images of her beautiful room, her desk, and her bookcase full of art supplies tormented her.

She leapt off the bench and tweaked Lily's toes, wiggling each one, making Lily giggle. She stroked Lily's feet, rubbing them gently and blowing on them.

After a while, she said, "Let me put your shoes on."

Lily grabbed a shoe. "Illy."

"Great!" Rose said. "You do one and I'll do one, okay?" Quickly, she put Lily's left shoe on her left foot. "You put that one on."

When both sandals were fastened, Rose helped Lily off the bench and took her hand. Lily toddled along beside her.

At McDonald's, Rose read the menu. What did babies eat? Lily had teeth, so maybe she would like what Rose liked.

Rose ordered chicken nuggets with honey mustard and fries and two milks.

The world got brighter as Lily filled herself up. A mama with a little girl sat at a table near them. The woman smiled at Rose and Lily.

Rose smiled back and sat up straighter, wanting to look like a good babysitter.

"How old is she?" the woman asked.

Rose had no idea—which felt *wrong* somehow. Everybody should know how old their sister was.

"How old are you, sweetie?" the woman asked Lily.

Lily held up five honey-mustard-covered fingers on one hand and one finger on the other hand.

The woman laughed. "Six, huh? She's so cute."

When she and Lily were through eating, Rose dumped their trash and took Lily into the restroom because Lily had honey mustard all over her dress. Rose rubbed it with wet toilet paper, but the toilet paper turned to pills. When she tried to lift Lily so she could splash water on the dress, they got tangled up and Lily slipped out of Rose's arms and banged her chin.

"I'm sorry!" Rose said.

Lily wailed.

"I'm *so* sorry, Lily!"

Lily shrieked, her face red.

"I didn't mean to," Rose said.

Lily's screams let Rose see all her teeth.

"Oh, poor Lily," Rose breathed.

Lily's face was purple now. She did a stomping dance and threw herself on the floor. When Rose tried to pick her up, Lily kicked, shrieking until her breath was gone and she lay silent and wide-eyed.

She wasn't breathing.

She was dying.

She couldn't die. Rose had just found her.

Lily caught her breath and began to scream again, kicking and arching her back.

Someone came in. "Help!" Rose said. "Something's wrong with my sister!"

The person, a teenager, looked at Lily. "Did she hurt herself?"

"She banged her chin on the sink."

"Maybe she's just throwing a fit."

"*Why?*"

The girl shrugged and rummaged in her purse. She stepped over Lily to get to the mirror. She had to yell to be heard. "She's two or three, right? They do that."

Lily *might* be two or three. Rose knelt beside Lily again. "Please stop, Lily."

Lily turned up the volume. The girl at the mirror rubbed gloss over her lips. "Just ignore her. She'll run down eventually."

Rose tried to tweak one of Lily's toes and Lily wailed so loud it made echoes.

The girl was leaving.

"*Why* do they throw fits?" Rose pleaded. "Other than because they just do."

"My little brother usually threw them for the fun of it. But sometimes he was tired. Or hungry. Or he didn't feel good." And the door closed behind her.

Rose sat on the floor, though it was dirty and streaked with water. She didn't like to think about how filthy Lily was getting. She'd need another bath. And clean clothes.

Rose wrapped her arms around her knees and waited.

Finally, Lily began to wind down and let Rose cuddle her. Rose looked at her chin. There was no mark. "Are you okay now?" she asked.

Lily nodded.

Lily seemed tired and crabby and sad as Rose unlocked the door and they went into the apartment. Rose had no idea what she was doing. She ached for Ama and home so much she thought she might disappear. But she was in charge, so she made herself say, "I wish I could make you feel better, Lily."

Rose put the cartons of milk from McDonald's in the nasty refrigerator. Then she turned to the piles of boxes on the table and chairs. She should find out if there was any more food in the apartment.

She set a box on the floor. "Do you want to see what's in the box, Lily?"

Solemnly, Lily came and peered into the box. "Bobble!" Her face lit up.

The bottle was like the ones Rose had fed her baby dolls with, only bigger. Lily snatched it and hugged it to her chest and began to jabber. All Rose understood was *Bobble, bobble!* She thrust it at Rose.

"You want me to fill it?"

"Bobble!"

It smelled sour when Rose unscrewed the top. "Let's wash

it first." She pointed to the chair that was still by the sink. "Will you help?"

Lily scrambled onto the chair.

When the bottle was clean and full of milk, Lily closed her mouth around the nipple and her eyes glazed over. She led Rose to the ratty bedding on the floor in front of the television.

Rose made a nest out of the bedding and snuggled beside Lily on the floor. Lily's eyes went to the television. She looked at Rose and pointed. Rose turned it on to a show for little kids. Lily's fingers found their way into Rose's hair and she began to squeeze and pull. It felt weird, but in a nice way. The way Lily looked up at Rose made her think of a sweet little bottle calf. The swell of love in Rose was so huge it made her dizzy, and then she felt the loss. Ama would be taking care of Peanutbutter now. As Lily's gaze shifted back to the television, Rose let the tears roll down her face. She felt like someone who had walked a hundred miles, outsmarted a two-headed pig, wrestled an octopus, and was still lost in a strange place. But Lily's sucking sounds and the bubbling of the bottle were soothing and Rose shut her eyes and took comfort from her baby sister.

#

Rose was folding an origami fortune-teller and Lily was cradling her newly filled bottle as if it were a baby when they heard the key in the door.

Iris's face darkened as she came through the door. "What's she doing with that thing?"

135

Lily scooted backward, her eyes big.

"Sheesh!" Iris strode across the room. As she snatched the bottle, Rose caught a greasy food smell from the bag Iris carried.

Lily's mouth began to quiver and her eyes filled with tears. She held out her arms to Rose. Lily felt so tiny and helpless. Being needed by a small, adorable critter filled Rose to overflowing. She glared at Iris.

"She's way too old for a bottle!" Iris said. "Where did it even come from?"

"I found it in that box." Rose pointed. "I didn't know she shouldn't have it. I'm not a real babysitter."

Iris sighed loudly and plunked the sack of food on the counter. "Obviously."

Trying to stifle her sobs, Lily clung to Rose.

"It's my fault she saw her bottle." Rose tried to keep her voice firm. "Like I said, I'm not a real babysitter. So I'm quitting." She hoped Iris didn't call her bluff because there was no way she'd leave Lily.

Iris looked at Rose. Lily clung tighter.

"I'm quitting unless you give her bottle back." She put steel into her voice. How did Iris know Lily was too old? Iris didn't seem like an encyclopedia of baby knowledge.

Iris didn't say anything.

"If you give it back, I might stay."

Iris rolled her eyes, but she left the bottle on the counter as she went into her bedroom and shut the door.

Rose carried Lily across the room. She let Lily grab the bottle and hug it close. Rose kissed Lily's head. "There now. Everything's okay," she murmured.

When Iris finally came out of the bedroom, Rose and Lily were having a picnic on the living room floor. Rose had spread a towel for a tablecloth. She didn't know if all the food in the sack was for them, and she didn't care. She'd opened the white cartons of takeout, and they were eating.

Lily was making an awful mess with the rice, but so was Rose. Maybe there were forks or spoons somewhere. Probably somewhere weird. The whole apartment was weird. Iris was weird.

Lily picked the peas out of the rice and put them in a pile. No wonder. They tasted like plastic. If Rose could take Lily to the garden and let her pick sugar snaps and eat them right there with ladybugs flying around, Lily would *love* peas. Fresh peas tasted like sunshine. And they smelled like heaven. Rose picked out her own peas and added them to the pile.

Lily watched her mother warily. She had hidden her bottle under the blanket.

Iris had changed clothes. As she swooshed past, Rose caught a flowery scent that set off alarm bells in Rose. Her mother's visit when Rose was little flashed in her memory and, as always, a piece was barely missing. Iris still wore her lashes, but the headband was gone. She looked pretty as she swung her purse over her shoulder.

"See you later," she said. And she was out the door.

Is this what *babysitting* meant? That Iris was going to fly in, change clothes, drop off a sack of food, and fly out again? Rose should unpack. Put things away. Get things organized so Lily didn't live in this mess.

A while later, Rose had finished giving Lily yet another bath when someone knocked. Dread that it might be Ama pounded against Rose's ribs. But Aunt Carol called from the hallway. Rose stood on a chair to see through the peephole. Aunt Carol was alone.

Rose opened the door.

"Thank goodness!" Aunt Carol pulled her into a hug. "I just got Tulip's message to look in on you. I've been in a big Realtors' meeting all day. Are you okay? Your grandmother is very worried, and I've been sent to calm the waters a little and get you home where you belong."

Lily came toddling into the room carrying her bottle. Her curls were damp from the bath and she looked very clean and smelled nice, which Rose was grateful for.

"This is my sister, Lily," Rose said.

"So I heard." Aunt Carol squatted in front of Lily.

Lily leaned against Rose.

"I brought you some things," Aunt Carol told Lily, patting a canvas tote. "These belonged to my little girl." She held the tote so Lily could see inside. "Shall we have a look?"

Aunt Carol sat in a kitchen chair. She let Lily take things out of the bag. Books. A family of tiny, flexible dolls in colorful clothes.

To Rose, Aunt Carol said, "Where's Iris?"

"I don't know. She came home and then left again."

"Have you looked after the little one all day?"

Rose nodded.

"How did it go?"

"Fine." But Rose was tired.

Lily was turning the pages of a board book.

"Do you think Maddy could help me babysit?" Rose asked.

"Oh, honey, you and Maddy can't take care of this little person all day, every day."

"Her name is Lily."

"Ose!" Lily said, looking up. She held the book for Rose to see.

"I thought maybe Maddy could come over sometimes and just hang out."

Aunt Carol sat with her feet together, her arms close to her side as if she didn't want to touch anything. "You mustn't get attached. Who knows what Iris will decide to do next?"

"I can't leave Lily in a place like this."

"Well, you're going to have to because you have to go home. And Tulip can't be expected to raise another child."

Expected. Rose supposed Ama had been expected to raise her. And it was hard taking care of babies. She understood that now.

Aunt Carol looked around the room, her eyes stopping on Lily. "I'm sorry you stumbled into this business when you're just a child yourself. You can't possibly understand," Aunt Carol said. "You must let your grandmother come and get you."

Rose shook her head. "No." She was exhausted, but there was no way she was leaving Lily.

Aunt Carol sighed. "Don't be silly, Rose. You can't stay *here*." Aunt Carol motioned at the mess.

"Maybe we could live with you and Uncle Thomas." They had a huge house.

"Oh." Aunt Carol drew her head back. "No. That wouldn't work. I'm sorry."

"I'll take care of Lily. I'll wash her and feed her and dress her—" Lily came to Rose and tugged her hand. "She can sleep with me. Everything."

Aunt Carol looked sad.

"You won't even know we're around," Rose said. She was begging and Ama said never to beg.

"We're leaving for England soon," Aunt Carol said. "But even if we weren't, you must go home to your grandmother because that's where you belong. And," she said, holding up a finger, "nobody can just *take* this little one even if they wanted to. Iris is her mother, and mothers have rights."

Rose sat on the floor and gathered Lily onto her lap. She put her hands over Lily's ears before she said, "But Iris doesn't *care*." She buried her face in Lily's curls. "I'm all Lily's got."

It was getting dusky in the room. Aunt Carol's white dress made her look like a stern angel perched in the chair, her wings folded tightly. Tonight Rose would tell Lily a story about an angel banished from heaven because her heart was closed tight as a fist. She wished Aunt Carol would go away.

Aunt Carol stood. "You can't spend the night alone here with the child. Iris isn't answering her phone, but I'll leave a message saying you and the little one are with me."

It was getting dark, and Iris might be gone for a long time. There would be voices in the hall and horns in the parking lot.

"I even went up to the attic and dug out Maddy's old car seat—hoping you'd come to our house for the night."

"Who's at your house?"

"Just me. Thomas and Maddy have gone to a Cardinals game. They're going to spend the night in St. Louis."

"Pinky swear there's nobody else at your house."

Aunt Carol hooked her pinky through Rose's.

#

Later, in Maddy's room, Aunt Carol tucked them in the way she always did, but it was Rose and Lily instead of Rose and Maddy. It was a relief to have a grown-up in charge for a while, even if Aunt Carol was kind of coldhearted.

Lily kept squirming and bonking Rose with her bottle.

Rose pretended to be asleep so Lily would go to sleep and Rose could be free for a while, even if just in her head.

"Ose," Lily said.

Rose didn't answer.

She felt Lily sit up.

Rose peeked. Lily's curls made a silhouette as she turned her head, looking first in one dark corner of the room, then the other.

Lily lay down with her face close to Rose's. "Ose," she whispered.

"Ose?" Lily sounded so alone—as if the world were huge and dark and dangerous and she was lost.

Rose's heart melted and she put her arms around her sister and pulled her close. She kissed Lily and rubbed her back. Before long, Lily was breathing evenly.

This was the second night Lily had fallen asleep in Rose's arms. What if Iris had gone away and left Lily with Rose, the same way she'd gone off and left Rose with Ama years ago? Earlier, when Iris had gotten all prettied up and had swished out, she'd acted like it was the first day of summer vacation. Maybe she wasn't coming back. Maybe she'd seen that Rose had loved Lily on sight and would take care of her. Rose felt more grown-up than her mother.

If Iris was gone for good, what would they do? They couldn't count on Aunt Carol and Uncle Thomas. Rose had read a book about children who lived in a museum. There wasn't a museum here, but there was a mall. They would need money. Rose had sixteen dollars from feeding the neighbors' dog while they went to Missouri to visit their kids at Easter, and Aunt Carol had paid her twenty-five dollars for folding origami place cards for the sorority Christmas party. And she'd won blue ribbons for her paper art in 4-H. Probably people would be glad to buy it. Great-aunt Harriet Jane had made a lot of money from her art.

She heard Aunt Carol talking to someone. Fearful of a double cross, her heart racing, she slipped out of bed and to the head of the stairs.

But Aunt Carol was only on the phone with Ama. "She's fine, Tulip. I'm keeping an eye on her." After a minute, she said, "Maybe it's good to let her care for the little one. She'll tire of it and be ready to come home." Aunt Carol listened. "I know you feel guilty. But none of us are perfect." She listened again. "Don't worry, she's safe here and I'll keep you posted. Remember this is Rose we're talking about." Aunt Carol laughed. "You've said yourself she's done a great job of raising you."

Tears sprang to Rose's eyes. She needed to get home to Ama. Ama's words still broke her heart, but Ama needed her too. But Lily was so small and helpless.

Rose got back into bed, but she couldn't sleep even though she was worn out. She didn't understand why Iris didn't see that she needed to make the apartment neat so they could find things. Why Iris didn't have real food in the refrigerator. Why she didn't have furniture so they could be comfortable. Why she didn't clean up messes so the place didn't smell. Weren't those things people naturally understood, the way Myrtle understood what she needed to do to take care of Ama and Rose and the farm? The way cows understood they needed to clean their newborn calves and let them nurse?

She sighed and gazed at the pale rectangle of light from the window. She longed for country darkness, for the sounds of tree frogs and coyotes.

·· eleven ··

W HEN Rose woke, Lily was crossways in the bed with one foot on Rose's stomach. Lily's diaper had leaked and the sheet was wet with pee. Maddy would be disgusted.

Rose eased out of bed and went to find Aunt Carol in the kitchen. Iris was there too, slumped over her phone. The way she looked like a wilted flower, still in yesterday's clothes, reminded Rose of something, but she wasn't sure what. It was kind of like this had all happened before, but it hadn't. The main thing was that Iris was here. The weight of worry about how to take care of Lily on her own lifted.

"We can't hang around," Iris said without looking up. "I have to sleep before I go to work at three."

Aunt Carol knew what Rose liked for breakfast and made her a buttered English muffin without asking. She also poured a little coffee into a cup of milk and handed it to Rose. She'd have given anything to wrap her arms around Ama and catch the smell of morning coffee on her breath.

While Rose was eating, Iris left the room and came back leading Lily, who looked cranky. She wore only a diaper and her sandals. Her eyes, when they came to Rose, were dull with sleep.

Rose ran up to Maddy's room and got her backpack, which she'd used for Lily's bottle, a few diapers, and a clean dress.

In the kitchen, Aunt Carol handed Rose a grocery bag. "Just a few nibbles," she said.

Iris was leading Lily to the door.

"Wait," Rose said, holding up the dress.

Iris looked impatient, but she stopped so Rose could put the dress on Lily.

Rose kissed Lily's curls as she smoothed the dress over her round belly. When Rose stood up, Lily touched herself and said, "Pitty?"

"Yes!" Rose said, clapping. "Pretty." Lily had learned a word.

As they left, Aunt Carol called, "I'll stop by later and see how you're doing."

When they were getting into the car, Rose saw there was no car seat in the back. "Where's the car seat?"

"I sold it," Iris said. "She's getting too big for one anyway."

"No, she isn't," Rose said. How could her mother be so dumb? Or so careless?

Rose got into the backseat with Lily. She pulled Lily onto her lap and fastened the seat belt over both of them; then she crossed her arms over her sister. Lily fit perfectly on her lap, like Rose was her special throne.

"Why don't you take better care of Lily?" Rose asked. She hated to hurt Iris's feelings, but couldn't Iris see that Lily was too small not to be in a car seat?

Iris's eyes did look hurt when she met Rose's gaze in the rearview mirror. "How do you mean?" she asked.

"Really?" Rose said.

Now Iris's eyes looked annoyed. "Forget it." She added, "Plus, how do you know about babies?"

"My dolls," Rose said. "I took care of my baby dolls. Didn't you play with dolls?"

"No."

"But I found yours. The ones in the bookcase that you were looking at Sunday."

"I didn't *play* with those," Iris said. "I *made* them. With Grandma Clara." She sighed. "Those were the best times of my life. I was truly happy when we were making dolls and she'd go on and on, telling me family stories."

"Yeah?" Rose said. Ama didn't tell family stories, except for the high points. And even those tended to come out only when Uncle Thomas was around and started telling them.

"Yeah," Iris said, smiling in the mirror. "I wish you could have heard some of them. She told me about her mother. Belle. The one with the angel in the cemetery. Grandma Clara said she was an awful mother." She lifted her shoulder in a shrug. "And other things. It was like as she got really old, Grandma Clara's filter wore out."

147

It felt weird to be having a real conversation with her mother. Iris had been an almost-empty box in Rose's brain. She'd been just a place on the family tree with a name inside it—and one memory with a piece missing.

"How old were you when Grandma Clara had her stroke?"

"Fourteen. I holed up for a week in my closet after it happened. I felt like I'd lost everything."

"But didn't you love the farm?" Rose asked. "The animals. All the stuff to do."

"Nope," Iris said.

"How could you not love the farm?"

Iris shrugged again. "My father's child, I guess."

Rose had never met her grandfather, but she didn't like him.

Iris said, "Or maybe I'm like Belle. Grandma Clara said her mother *hated* the farm. I didn't hate it. It just didn't mean anything to me. *Nada*."

Lily had gone back to sleep. Her head lolled against Rose's arm, her body slack. It felt strange, like Lily was part of her.

"You kept Lily," Rose said. "Why didn't you keep me?"

Iris glanced at her in the mirror. "I was too young. And doing all kinds of dumb stuff."

Iris struck Rose as still too young.

"Then why did you have me?"

"Blame my best friend, Jodi. She was older and already had a kid. She said after she had her baby, people treated her more grown-up. So I thought maybe having a baby might make me more grown-up. And I kind of wanted somebody to love. Somebody to love me. I was lonesome." The back of her neck turned pink. She rushed on, "After I found out you were on the way, I dropped out of school and got a job at McDonald's. Jodi moved out of her parents' house with her little girl, and we got an apartment. I stopped doing the stupid stuff I'd been doing."

"Ama didn't know about me?" Rose didn't like the idea of existing even in her mother's womb without Ama knowing about her.

"No. I was afraid Grandma Clara would find out and be disappointed in me. Ma tried to call me a lot. Sometimes Dad did, but he was living with his honey—a student, like Ma back in the day—and I don't think I meant a thing to him anymore. I meant something to Ma. But looking back, she was wrapped up in her own troubles."

Ama's life seemed so calm and peaceful and happy now. It was hard for Rose to believe what Iris said about Ama.

"Do you want to hear this whole long story, really?" Iris asked.

Rose was desperate to hear it. There were parts that felt so not right, but she wanted to know. It was *her* story.

"Well, Jodi let her boyfriend move in to help with rent, and things were okay. Her little girl started staying mainly with her parents. After a while, I could feel you moving around."

That was so strange for Rose to hear. She felt her face get hot.

"I started taking mommy-baby classes at the hospital and feeling like maybe something good was going to happen to me, finally. Somehow, magically, I'd have you and be a good mother—much better than my mother, I thought—and we'd love each other and live happily ever after. We would be perfect, like those pictures of mamas and babies you see in magazines. Jodi was in the delivery room with me. When I left the hospital, I went back to the apartment."

The light changed then, and so did Iris's voice. "But I felt so sad and so empty. It wasn't like in the magazines. I couldn't get out of bed. I couldn't take care of you." Her eyes flicked to Rose's. "I'm sorry," she said. "Our rosy dream went dark."

Rose felt an ache for her mother. She wanted to say *It's okay. I was perfectly happy with Ama*, but she didn't.

"I went back to old habits. And one day when I was happy and high I had a wonderful revelation. I should give you to Ma and Grandma Clara! In my fog, I wasn't remembering that Grandma Clara was in a bad way and so was Ma. I just knew Grandma Clara loved kids and would be thrilled to have you. So I put you in your carrier and took you to Ma like a house-warming present. And I split."

"And Ama didn't know anything about me before that?"

"Nope."

"Holy cow." Ama's cruel words Sunday night still hurt a lot, but things were clearer.

"In my defense," Iris said, "abandoning your kid does run in the family."

"No, it doesn't." Rose knew the whole family tree.

"Ma never told you?"

"No." Rose wanted to stop talking. She couldn't bear to know who else had done it.

Plus, they were turning into the parking lot. Glad to end the conversation, Rose woke up Lily and helped her out of the car.

In the apartment, the muffled thud of music next door came through the wall.

Iris suddenly looked as if she might fall asleep standing up. "I've got my alarm set for two o'clock." And she went into her bedroom and shut the door.

Lily looked at Rose. "Bobble," she said.

Rose took the bottle out of the plastic bag, washed it, and filled it with milk, which they were almost out of. Lily lay down in front of the TV.

Rose peeked inside the bag Aunt Carol had sent. There were oranges and grapes and peanut butter sandwiches. And a folded piece of paper.

The second Rose unfolded it, she knew the note was from Ama. Rose folded it back up. Her heart was still broken. But Ama had said she was sorry. Maybe the note said Lily could come and live with them. With hope high in her throat, Rose unfolded the paper again.

Rose, I wasn't speaking to you when I said those harsh words. I'm sorry you heard them. Peanutbutter wonders what has happened to you. Myrtle misses you. I miss you. Please come home. Love, Ama

Nothing about Lily, who looked as sad as Rose felt.

"I know!" Rose said, swallowing the lump in her throat and forcing a happy voice. "Let's play house. Want to?"

Lily seemed puzzled, but she nodded, put her bottle down, and got up.

"Okay." Rose led Lily to the junky room with the bare mattress on the floor.

First, they sorted through the mishmash of stuff strewn all over the place. Lily helped Rose fold the towels, touching her nose to Rose's when the corners met. Rose put the bottle of pills, the Kleenex, and the diapers on a shelf in the bathroom. She stored the plastic bucket under the kitchen sink. She left the elephant piñata, broken only a little, in the room.

They piled all the grown-up clothes in front of Iris's door. Lily carried the items and tossed them into the pile, looking to Rose for approval.

After a while, Lily's curls began to mat to her neck. Rose was hot too, but the only air conditioner was humming away behind Iris's closed door.

Rose tried to open the bedroom window. She pushed hard.

When nothing happened, she pushed harder. The harder she pushed, the hotter she got.

She dragged a chair into the bedroom and stood on it. She flung her shoulder against the window. With a pop, it came free and she cranked it wide open. Lily lifted her face to the puff of air.

"Does that feel good?" Rose asked.

Lily beamed.

"Back to work," Rose said, ruffling Lily's hair.

The stains on the mattress were disgusting, so Rose heaved the mattress over. The other side was cleaner. She dragged the mattress to cover the carpet stain, which looked kind of like a pig.

She leaned the piñata against the wall. "Does it look pretty there?" she asked Lily.

"Pitty."

They could use the gold-painted basket for Lily's clothes, if Rose ever found them in the clutter of Iris's room. While Iris was at work, Rose would look for them. And she'd steal a pillow off Iris's bed for herself. Meanwhile, she put the little football-shaped pillow on the mattress for Lily. And she brought in her backpack and placed it beside the bed.

Rose stood in the doorway, admiring their work. The room was neat. She and Lily carried in the books and tiny dolls from Aunt Carol and lined them up along the wall with the piñata.

This room was their safe and cozy home. They wouldn't let in anyone else without permission.

"Shall we read a book?" she asked Lily.

Lily looked puzzled.

"Book," Rose said, picking one up.

As they sat on the mattress turning pages, Lily looked for the mouse hidden in each illustration. Rose told her over and over, "Mouse!"

When they were done, Rose gave her the book. "Can you find the mouse?"

Lily turned the pages, putting her finger on the mouse. At the end, she closed the book and said, "Book."

Rose hugged her. "Homeric!"

\#

That afternoon, when Iris passed their room on the way to the kitchen, she glanced in and stopped, standing in the doorway. Rose kept cutting a butterfly out of the empty cereal box.

Iris came in.

"Please knock," Rose said.

"The door is open."

"Because we get hot if it's closed. This room is our house. You have to say *knock, knock*."

Iris shook her head. But she said, "Knock, knock."

"Come in." Rose snipped the butterfly free and let it fall into the pile on the floor.

"What the heck are you doing?"

"Decorating."

Lily, with tape in her hair and tangled around one wrist, was trying to stick a yellow star to the wall.

The stars and moon, butterflies, bees, and flowers weren't as high on the wall as Rose would have liked, but Lily was having a good time. Rose kept snipping. She cut out a green garden snake. She felt Iris watching.

As Rose snipped out a whole family of garden snakes from a grocery store flyer she'd found in a box, Iris came closer.

"Where did you find the scissors?" she asked, sitting on the floor.

"They were in my backpack," Rose said, keeping her face bent over her work.

Lily picked a green squiggle from the pile of Rose's cuttings. "Dis?" she asked.

"Snake," Rose said, making a wiggle motion with her hand, then tearing off a piece of tape for Lily.

"Nake," Lily said, going to the wall.

"Maybe we could take turns with the scissors?" Iris said.

"Don't you have any?"

"No."

What kind of person had no scissors?

A person like her mother. A person who didn't think very far ahead.

Rose handed the scissors to Iris. As Iris picked up a scrap of paper and began to cut, Rose noticed how similar their hands were.

She asked the question she'd been trying not to think about all day. "Was Ama the person who went off and left a baby?"

"No." Iris looked shocked. "It was Harriet Jane. Lotus."

Great-aunt Harriet Jane? The world traveler who spoke Italian? The one who saved the farm?

"Grandma Clara told me all about it when I was your age. That's what I meant about her filter being broken."

Rose shook her head. Great-aunts were supposed to be responsible and dignified. Even hippie great-aunts. "So what happened to the baby?"

"She became a farmer." Iris gave Rose a long look.

"What?"

"Ma. She's Harriet Jane's daughter."

"No, she's not. Ama is Harriet Jane's baby sister. Ama helped me make the family tree for my oral report."

Iris put down the scissors, shaking her head. "Two things families couldn't own back in the day. Unwed mothers and mental illness."

Rose wasn't listening to what Iris was saying. Why had Ama lied when they made the family tree?

"Ask Ama," Iris said.

Just then, her phone vibrated and she left the room to talk.

When Lily came to get another snipping, Rose caught her and pulled her onto her lap and hugged her. Sometimes it was awful the way kids were treated by grown-ups. Lily melted into Rose's arms at first, but not for long. She squirmed and said,

"Nake." She took another snake from the stack and went to the wall.

"Idiots!" Iris said, getting off the phone. "They don't want me today after all. But I have to be there at eight thirty in the morning."

"Why would Ama make the family tree wrong?" Rose hated to use the *L*-word, but she did. "Why would she lie to me?"

"You should probably talk to her about it," Iris said.

Rose wasn't talking to Ama right now. But family trees were important, and she didn't like having it all wrong.

Iris went into the kitchen. Rose heard her open a soft drink. Didn't she ever eat? Rose and Lily had shared an orange and the sandwiches and eaten several grapes, though Lily spat out the skins. And Rose had used the change from the twenty-dollar bill yesterday to walk to McDonald's with Lily for more milk.

Lily didn't suck on her bottle much. She mainly helped Rose wash and dry it, hid it, checked on it, talked to it, cuddled it. Maddy still had a zillion dolls in the back of her closet. Why hadn't Aunt Carol brought a real baby doll instead of the tiny figures? Lily would love a real baby doll.

"Knock, knock."

Rose didn't look up.

"Knock, knock," Iris said again.

"What?" Rose said. She wished Iris hadn't told her about Harriet Jane.

"I have an idea. I could cut and style your hair."

"Why?"

"It's fun. And you don't want to wear bangs and a ponytail forever."

Why wouldn't she?—though Maddy had been going to Aunt Carol's stylist.

"I'm really very good at cuts," Iris said. "When I stay in one place long enough, I develop a following." Iris's freckles darkened when she blushed. "Believe it or not."

But Rose had always had bangs and a ponytail. When her bangs got in her eyes, Ama trimmed them. When her ends got ragged, Ama evened them. Longing washed over Rose.

"Ose," Lily said. She looked worried.

Rose scrubbed away the tears, hoping Iris hadn't seen.

A few minutes later, Rose bent over the bathroom sink while Iris shampooed her hair. Iris's strong fingers relaxed Rose's scalp so much she felt floaty.

"Okay," Iris said as she worked. "Tell me five things about yourself." Her voice sounded like Maddy's in the dark. Mysterious. Different.

"Why?"

"So I know how to cut and style your hair."

"What kind of things?"

"Any old thing at all. How tall you are. Your favorite food. Where you want to be in ten years. Who you love most. Your first pet's name."

This was silly, yet the feeling of Iris's fingers on her scalp sort of hypnotized her into going along. "I'm ten years old." But her own mother knew that. "My first and only pet's name is Myrtle." Though Myrtle was way more than a pet. "I'm going to be some kind of artist when I grow up. And I can do anything I set my mind to." That was only four, but she didn't know what else to say.

"Umm," Iris said, rinsing Rose's hair. "I can work with that."

Whatever that meant.

Iris toweled Rose's hair a little, then massaged in something that smelled like roses, then rinsed again. Iris relaxed against her mother's body. The closeness and fragrance were familiar, as if this had happened before. Rose shivered as her mother wrapped a towel around her head.

She opened her eyes. In the mirror, with the towel making a turban, she looked like Iris. She took off the towel. "I've changed my mind."

"But I'm an excellent stylist," Iris said.

"Ama says cutting hair dulls scissors. I don't want my scissors dulled."

"Obviously, Ma knows everything. If you don't believe me, just ask her."

"Why don't you like her?"

"Because I could never do anything right as far as she was concerned."

Rose shook out her hair and ran her fingers through her bangs.

Iris watched her in the mirror. "But she thinks you make the sun rise in the morning and set in the evening."

Rose couldn't find her voice because Iris's words hurt so much. Finally, she whispered, "I think the same thing about her."

"So you need to kiss and make up," Iris said.

"But how could she give me away to strangers?"

Iris laughed. "Well, she didn't follow through."

Rose tried to glare at Iris, but tears flooded her eyes. Iris didn't know how Ama's words made her feel.

Iris sat on the edge of the tub. "Ma used to tell me what I didn't know couldn't hurt me."

"She tells me that too."

"And you didn't need to know that." Iris's face showed sympathy that made Rose feel even worse because she didn't want to like Iris very much. "Believe me," Iris said, "I heard way more than I needed to know when I was a kid because of that stupid listening post. Ma and Larry used to say horrible things to each other."

"Why did you call your dad by his first name?"

"Because he wanted me to. My friends thought it was so cool. They thought *he* was so cool." Iris rolled her eyes. "Did you know he was one of Ma's college professors? Have you ever seen pictures of Ma when she was in college?"

"She was Miss Southern Illinois University 1987." Ama let Rose and Maddy dress up in her beauty contest sash.

"Yeah. Plus she inherited money from Lotus. I imagine a lot of guys might have been happy to marry her. And she settled on the wrong one. She was probably flattered to get romantic attention from a professor."

Rose had seen pictures of him. He had dark hair and dark eyes and was about Ama's height. His expressions seemed to say *I know more than you*. Rose was glad he was gone. She wouldn't want somebody looking at her like that every day.

Rose couldn't shake off the familiar, shivery feeling she'd had when she was leaning against Iris at the sink. "That time you came to visit I was really little—I kind of remember it, and I kind of don't. What happened?"

Iris leaned against the doorframe. "Well, it wasn't a carefully planned visit. As in Mom had no idea I was coming. I hadn't been in touch since I parked you on her doorstep. But one night I was out with friends and got really happy and decided I should come and see you. I jumped in the car and drove from Kentucky. I felt like I was flying through the night. I was lucky I didn't get pulled over." Iris's face flushed. "I remember the sun coming up just east of town, and I took it as a sign my visit was meant to be." Her freckles grew darker. "It was stupid, but it seemed like a good idea at the time."

The part of the visit Rose remembered was waking up and going into the kitchen to see the new puppy and sit on Ama's lap, like she always did first thing in the morning. But Ama hadn't been in the kitchen.

"When I got there," Iris said, "I just walked in. The house was quiet, so I sat down at the kitchen table. And in a few minutes, you came toddling in. You were so adorable. You were surprised I wasn't Ma, but I managed to coax you to sit on my lap. Your hair was all tangled up, and I was combing it with my fingers when Ma came in with a puppy and started screaming at me."

The cloud lifted from the memory. Rose had sat on the pretty lady's lap. The pretty lady had been gentle and she smelled good. And Rose liked to have her hair petted.

That was why Ama screamed. Because Rose shouldn't have been on the pretty lady's lap. It was like the electric fence or getting too close to the cows. Dangerous.

Rose felt a little dizzy. Iris was still talking but Rose was swamped with her own thoughts. When had she figured out the pretty lady was her mother?

"I think Ma was afraid I'd come to take you, and by then you were the most important thing in the world to her. I'd really just come to say hello. But right after that, she started the adoption process."

Iris stood staring into space. "Let's face it. Ma and I never got along great. And after that blowup when she saw you on my lap, I decided the best thing for me to do was just disappear from your lives. So I did."

She suddenly looked as tired as Rose felt.

Iris said, "Grandma Clara had this silly riddle. You want to hear?"

Rose nodded.

"Pete and Repeat were sitting on a fence. Pete fell off and who was left?"

"Repeat," Rose answered.

"Pete and Repeat were sitting on a fence. Pete fell off and who was left?"

Rose groaned. "That's lame."

"But it was kind of like she was predicting my life."

That was sad.

Rose realized she'd forgotten about Lily for a few minutes. And Lily was being awfully quiet. "I need to check on Lily," she said, brushing past Iris.

"But Grandma Clara also said we never know how life is going to turn out," Iris added.

In their bedroom, Lily was asleep on the mattress, cradling the mouse book.

"I'm going to take a shower," Iris announced, starting to close the bathroom door.

"Wait," Rose said. "Did you know the surprise lily is Ama's favorite flower?"

Iris nodded.

"Is that why you named Lily Lily?"

Iris nodded again.

"Why did you name me Rose?"

"I needed a flower name, and I love roses. By the time Lily came along, I wasn't so mad at Ma anymore. I thought it might be nice."

Iris shut the door then and the shower went on.

Rose stretched out beside Lily and stared at the ceiling. She should have suspected there was something wrong with the family tree. Tulip, Iris, and Rose belonged under Lotus. She'd learned a lot from her mother today.

Maybe Iris wasn't as bad as Rose thought. But she didn't take good care of Lily, so Rose really was going to have to do that. But Iris could help. She could buy sheets for Lily and Rose's bed. And she could take Rose to the library to get a library card. She could buy real food. And Lily needed nicer clothes. Rose could tell her mother what she needed to do.

·· twelve ··

ROSE had been dreaming about Myrtle leaping onto her bed. But Rose wasn't in her bed. She was on a floor and the light was dim. Was it morning or evening? Her lips felt stuck together, and she was very hot. And it wasn't Myrtle beside her. It was her sister. Lily's mouth was open a little and she drooled.

Rose felt weird—as if she were in some foggy dreamlike place between the farm and here with her sister. A man, his voice hard, was talking. Rose sat up, licking her lips, trying to get completely awake.

The man was asking Iris about when she'd lived in Kentucky. When Iris answered, her voice was so low Rose couldn't make out the words, but Iris sounded upset, like maybe she was crying.

Should Rose go out and see what was wrong?

When the man mentioned innocent children, Iris cried, "I know, I *know!*"—her voice rising through her tears.

Did this have something to do with Lily? Rose's hand went to Lily, feeling the rise and fall of her breath.

Then the man said he was taking Iris into custody for some kind of theft.

His words took Rose's breath away. Had Iris stolen Lily?

"I'll take you to a federal holding facility," the man was saying. "You'll be locked up there until you can appear before a judge for arraignment."

Rose felt as if she'd been spun around too fast. She didn't understand the big words, but Iris was going to jail and it had something to do with Lily.

When Iris passed their door on her way down the hall, she glanced at Rose out of the corner of her eye and brushed her lips in a *be quiet* motion without turning her head.

Rose heard her grabbing some things in the bedroom; then Iris went into the bathroom. She turned so she and Rose were facing each other across the hall. Iris's face was terrified as she put her finger to her lips again. Her hand trembled. She mouthed, *Call Ma.*

Then she returned to the living room. "I'm ready now," she said, sounding as if the world had ended.

The door opened and closed, and they were gone.

Everything had happened so fast. Rose's heart was pounding as if she were chasing Iris down the hall. Yet she felt glued to the bed.

If Lily was stolen, that meant she wasn't Rose's sister. If she was stolen, might Rose go to jail if she didn't give Lily back? Would the man hurt Iris? Would Iris be safe in jail?

Eventually, thirst drove Rose to move. She felt like she could drink a swimming pool. She found a plastic cup in the kitchen and filled it from the tap and drank, refilling it three times.

Iris had said to call Ama, but Rose didn't have a phone. And even if she did, Ama wouldn't have anything to do with Lily. And if Lily was stolen, they might have to give her back anyway, and Rose couldn't possibly do that because Lily needed her. Rose had found her and was keeping her.

The sun was setting behind the buildings across the parking lot. As the apartment grew dimmer, Rose felt more scared.

She drifted back to their room, a knot in her throat. She sat on the floor and leaned against the wall, hugging her knees and staring at Lily. Why would Iris, who hadn't wanted her own child, steal someone else's? Did Lily have a family worrying about her?

Rose scooted closer to the mattress and studied Lily. The light was dim, but even outside in the sunshine, there was nothing about Lily that looked like Rose. Ama said the Lovells all had skin as pale as buttermilk. Lily's skin looked like coffee had been poured into the buttermilk. The Lovells had blond hair and blue eyes. Lily had dark hair and brown eyes. Yet even that first night in the apartment, when Rose didn't know if Lily was a boy or a girl, she'd had the feeling of two people who belonged together coming together. Lily and Rose.

Rose heard a tapping at the door and recognized Aunt

Carol's voice. She didn't know if she was glad to see her or not. She felt like she didn't know anything but was responsible for everything.

When Rose opened the door, Aunt Carol carried in a grocery sack. "I just stopped by to say hello," she said. "Why aren't there any lights on? Where is everybody?"

"Shhhhh," Rose whispered. "Iris and Lily are napping." If Aunt Carol knew Iris was in jail, she'd take charge and Lily and Rose would be separated.

Aunt Carol spoke more quietly. "Is everything okay, Rose?"

"Just fine," Rose said, making herself sound excited. "Iris needed a quick nap after work. We're going out to eat when they wake up."

"That sounds nice," Aunt Carol said.

Aunt Carol put the grocery bag on the kitchen counter. "I brought a few things for your dinner. In case you didn't have other plans," she added cheerfully.

"Thank you."

Aunt Carol put both hands on Rose's shoulders. "Rose, we're leaving for England tomorrow, so I won't be looking in on you again. Tulip is coming to get you bright and early in the morning. She's going to call Iris this evening to tell her."

Aunt Carol watched Rose, waiting for her to say something, but Rose's thoughts were flying in a million directions. She had to take Lily and run. Tonight.

Aunt Carol kept looking at her.

Rose nodded and said, "Babysitting is hard work."

Aunt Carol patted Rose's shoulder. "I knew you'd come around. By the time we get home next month this will all be forgotten. You'll be Maddy's sweet little country cousin again and everything will be back to normal."

"Yes," Rose said. "I hope you have a nice time in England." She wanted Aunt Carol to hurry up and leave.

Aunt Carol gave her a hug. "When Iris gets up, tell her I said hello."

"Okay."

After Aunt Carol left, Rose slumped against the door, but only for a few seconds.

Then she turned on the kitchen light and looked in the grocery sack. Aunt Carol had brought bread, a plastic container with thick slices of smoked ham, and a container of her homemade baked beans.

When Lily woke up, they would eat and then pack the leftovers. Plus, they should pack the peanut butter. And the chicken nuggets. And the two little cartons of milk that were left. And the bags of stale chips.

They'd need to pack Lily's bottle too. And they mustn't forget her diapers. Lily's books and toys. Her clothes.

Rose rushed into Iris's room and flipped on the light. She was pawing through the pile where she'd found the little red sundress yesterday when Lily bumped her. She was red-faced and scowling like the most miserable baby on the planet. She shoved Rose.

"Hey! Why are you pushing me?"

Lily scowled worse and pushed her again. This time Rose ended up sitting on the side of the mattress. When Lily scrambled into her lap as if a bad dream were chasing her, Rose's arms went around Lily and she hugged her. Lily snuggled closer.

Having her sweaty little sister in her arms—and Rose knew Lily *had to be* her sister (Iris must have stolen something else, and that was why she was in jail)—Rose felt better about everything.

After a while, Lily leaned back and gazed at Rose. Her face was still flushed with heat, but she smiled and her eyes shone. "Ose," she said, as if Rose were the finest thing on the planet.

"Lily," Rose said, looking into her sister's eyes.

"Book," Lily said, getting up and toddling off.

Rose went back to looking for clothes that weren't stained and didn't smell bad and looked as if they might fit.

They would have a lot to carry.

What about bedding?

She wished she knew for sure where they were going, but the most important thing was just to get out of here before Ama came.

If they went to the mall, there was a Penney's store with a pretty made-up bed. But Rose wouldn't be able to sleep out in the open like that, wondering if a security guard might discover them. They could probably use the store's blankets and pillows in a hiding place behind a counter or under a table.

Or in the dressing room! Rose had tried on bathing suits at Penney's last summer, and the stall in the dressing room had been very nice, with a door, and carpet, and just enough room for her and Lily to spread a blanket and sleep. Nobody would look in there after the store closed. But the floor would smell like feet, and there wouldn't be fresh air.

Lily came in with the book about the mouse and patted the mattress for Rose to sit down. Although it was hard to keep her mind off all the things she needed to do, Rose read to Lily. It was too late to move tonight because the mall would be closed by the time they got there. But they had to be long gone before Ama came in the morning.

Rose tried to stay patient, even when Lily insisted on turning pages backward to see if the mouse was still there. When Rose finally got to the end, she folded a tiny origami mouse to distract Lily, who took it away to show to her bottle.

Rose heard her babbling, her voice rising and falling, as Rose went back to looking for clothes.

She had no idea how they were going to get to the mall with all their stuff. Maybe the old man they'd seen sitting in the car that first morning would take them. But maybe he didn't sit in his car every day. Or maybe he wasn't a good driver and would smash into something. Plus, he was a stranger, and they shouldn't get into a car with a stranger.

Her stomach growled, reminding her they needed to eat. She spread a towel on the floor in the living room again and dipped Aunt Carol's baked beans into plastic cups. And she made ham sandwiches.

As they ate, Lily's eyes kept going to the TV even though it wasn't on.

"We're going to have lots of stuff to carry when we leave," Rose said. "Do you think you can walk all the way to the mall?"

Lily's eyes came to Rose's.

"I won't be able to carry you too," Rose said.

Lily shook her head and went back to gazing at the blank television.

Rose ate her sandwich, thinking about Aunt Carol, Uncle Thomas, and Maddy. Rose wouldn't get to say goodbye to Maddy.

Lily made a strangled, hacking sound. Her face was red and her eyes were watering. She pulled a wad of half-chewed ham out of her mouth, but she kept choking.

"Hold your arms up," Rose said, holding her own up. "Like this."

But Lily kept taking chunks of meat out of her mouth and getting redder and redder in the face. Her eyes filled with panic.

Rose leapt to her feet. Kneeling behind Lily, she lifted her upright. She should have known Lily didn't have enough teeth to chew ham. Maddy would have known.

4-H, she thought. "Here." She wrapped her arms around Lily and used her hands to push in what she hoped was the right place on Lily's tummy.

A little chunk flew out of Lily's mouth and landed on the towel. Lily sucked a clear breath.

In relief, Rose flopped to the floor and gathered Lily onto her lap, kissing her greasy face again and again. "Please don't need CPR," she said. "Please, please, please. I don't know how to do that."

Lily struggled free and put her hands on Rose's cheeks. "Ose," she said.

"What?"

"Ose."

"Yes." Rose took her sticky hands. "Don't worry. I'm not going anyplace. At least, not without you." She gave Lily one more hug.

Lily went back to eating the beans out of the plastic cup, and Rose went back to thinking about the trip to the mall.

They could try to walk with all their stuff, but it was a long way. What if Lily got tired and cranky and started screeching like a barn owl? Somebody might think Rose was hurting her. And for sure they would be noticed.

Lily held out her empty cup.

"Do you want more?" Rose asked.

Lily nodded.

"Say *More beans, please*."

Lily waggled the cup.

"You have to learn to talk, Lily." Rose pointed to her own beans. "Beans." She looked at Lily, waiting.

"Beans," Rose said again. "Beans." She pointed and looked at Lily.

"Bees?" Lily said.

Rose clapped. "Yes! Beans, beans, beans!"

"Bees, bees, bees," Lily said, clapping.

Rose gave her more beans. Lily was very smart. To make sure, Rose pointed to the beans and raised her eyebrows at Lily.

"Bees," Lily said.

Rose nodded. "Good."

Later, when Rose was cleaning up the disgusting pieces of mauled ham that Lily had choked on and was washing food off Lily's face and hands, she noticed what Lily was clutching in her beany fist.

The answer to their problem. Iris's car keys.

The car could hold all their stuff. They could go wherever they needed to go in the car.

They could *live* in the car.

She scooped up the keys and shook them like a tambourine. "Keys, keys, keys!"

"Keys!" Lily said.

Rose kissed her, not minding her bean-smeared face. "You are so smart."

·· thirteen ··

LILY was almost asleep. Rose was murmuring whatever she could think of, making it sound like a bedtime story. Lily probably didn't know what Rose was saying anyway. Lily needed to go to sleep so Rose could pack the car and make their getaway in absolute silence.

"You're learning more words all the time," Rose said softly. She didn't mention them, lest they pull Lily back from the edge of sleep. *"B-o-o-k, m-o-u-s-e, b-e-a-n-s."* In the dark, she felt Lily loosen her grip on her bottle. "And now you are *a-s-l-e-e-p,*" Rose whispered.

She eased away and went to the window. Iris's car, with its squashed front, sat waiting under a parking lot light. It looked angry and terrifying, but it was their only hope.

In Iris's room, she found a box the right size to hold Lily's clothes and diapers. She felt guilty messing with Iris's stuff, but she needed the box so she dumped it. She also needed something to pack their food into, so she dumped another box. When a few pictures stuck to the bottom, Rose pulled them loose.

One was of a teenage Iris, her belly huge, clowning with a

girlfriend. Rose wondered if it was the best friend her mother had talked about. She studied the photo. She was inside that big belly. She'd never thought of herself like that. Really small, not knowing anything yet, not even where she was. All folded up tight in there.

She almost took the snapshot because she didn't think Iris was coming back for a long time—maybe not ever. But after a minute, she let it fall onto the pile of Iris's stuff.

In the kitchen, she packed food. Then she gathered Lily's toys and books and a pillow from Iris's bed. Because it was summer, they wouldn't have to worry about getting cold at night. And by winter, she'd have money from her paper art to buy blankets and everything they'd need.

She felt how late it was. The music in the apartment next door had stopped. She looked through the peephole. The hall was empty. Taking Iris's keys and the gold basket full of Lily's toys, she swung her backpack over her shoulder. Everything was quiet behind the apartment doors as she hurried down the hall.

Outside, the air felt heavenly. She looked up, hoping to see the polestar, but in town, even in the middle of the night, there was too much light for stars.

The closer she got, the scarier Iris's car looked. Ama's car had been friendly and familiar because Rose had ridden in it and watched Ama drive it for years. Plus, Ama had slowly led the way that day after school, and all Rose had to do was follow.

And at the end, Ama had been there to say *Homeric!* And Myrtle had given Rose kisses.

Tears sprang to Rose's eyes. It was just her and Lily now, on their own. She kept on walking across the parking lot.

The car was unlocked. Rose put her backpack and the basket on the floor of the backseat and shut the door quietly, her hands trembling.

Suddenly afraid Lily might have awakened, Rose rushed back. But the apartment was quiet and Lily was sleeping.

She made a second trip, jittery as a grasshopper. She carried the box of food with her pillow on top. This time, a dog whined and yipped from behind a door. Maybe he smelled the ham. When Rose rushed down the hall, the dog went quiet.

The third trip was for Lily's clothing.

As the car filled with their things, it began to feel more familiar, but she didn't know if she could drive it. Were all cars the same?

Back inside the apartment for the last time, there was nothing left but her baby sister, Lily's bottle, and her little football pillow.

In their bedroom, she whispered in Lily's ear, "You stay asleep. I'll put you in the car. I'll make a nest for you in the backseat and when you wake up, we'll be in a whole different place. Just you and me."

Then, knowing she and Lily were going to leave forever, she went back to Iris's room and found the picture of Iris with her big stomach. She slipped the snapshot into her pocket.

She wrapped her arms around Lily, who was much heavier asleep than awake. Rose stumbled and Lily's bottle fell to the floor. Rose squatted, reaching for the bottle, and almost dropped her sister, who was like a beanbag, her weight shifting when Rose moved. Rose snatched the bottle and then used her leg to boost Lily up. Lily's head lolled on Rose's shoulder. Rose looked at the football pillow. There was no way she could get it. Lily could share Rose's pillow.

She was just about to open the door when someone pounded on it. Her heart bounced. Had the man who took Iris come back for Lily?

Then she heard the door in the next apartment open and the sound of voices. Then the door closed and the people were inside the apartment. She nearly toppled over with relief. Quickly, she went out the door, shut it behind her, and rushed along the hall, down the steps, and outside.

They were free.

She thought the fresh air might wake Lily, but Lily was so floppy her head bounced with every step Rose took. When Rose laid her sister down in the backseat, Lily stirred, opened her eyes a crack, and then closed them. Rose tucked her bottle beside her.

Rose arranged her backpack so it put her high enough to see and forward enough to reach the pedals. Thank goodness, Iris's car was like Ama's—one pedal to go and one to slow.

The letters for the gears were the same too. P and D were

the only two Rose knew how to use. P was for not moving, and D was for moving. She'd watched Ama enough to know that R was for going backward, but Rose hoped she didn't need to do that.

She found a key on Iris's key ring that fit in the keyhole. Closing her eyes, she turned it. When the beast leapt to life, a sound like a tiny scream escaped Rose.

··fourteen··

RYING to stay between the lines made Rose sick to her stomach. Terror caused her to turn the steering wheel too little or too much, and the car made big scary moves or hardly did anything at all. She tried to go slow but sometimes her foot shook so hard she shot ahead and her heart nearly came out her throat. And it was so hard to see in the dark.

When a horn blared behind her she jumped and let go of the wheel as she whirled around to look. Headlights were shining in her face, and she yelled because she thought the car was going to hit them. It swerved past, honking even more.

Lily stirred in the backseat.

No, no, no, go back to sleep! Rose had to concentrate. There was another car behind her now, and she didn't want to get honked at again. Hoping she didn't crash, she made her first turn, but the car honked at her anyway.

She had to look out for parked cars, garbage cans lining the street, and stop signs.

A car pulled out of a driveway right in front of her! Was the driver blind? Her foot got tangled up trying to get on the brake. The other car sped away, honking again.

Rose was so hot and pressured she thought she might explode. She reached for the control pad to open the windows and it wasn't there.

"Turn your lights on, fella!" somebody yelled as a car passed her.

Did they mean her?

Was that the problem—why people didn't see her? Why she couldn't see? But she didn't know how to turn the lights on.

There was a convenience store coming up, and she didn't see any other cars so she steered across the street and into the parking lot. She moved the gearshift to P and turned off the engine. The store was closed and she had the parking lot to herself. Her hands were trembling so hard when she took them off the wheel, she gripped the wheel again. What a stupid thing she'd done.

She pushed her book bag away and got out of the car. Her skin tingled as the air dried her clammy body. Even her hair was sweating. Her knees were shaking. She looked up at the sky. She'd feel better if she could see the polestar, but she didn't even know which way was north anymore.

"Ose?" Lily was sitting up, looking at her.

Rose opened the back door and picked Lily up, hugging her. She kissed Lily's hair and squeezed her closer. What if she'd crashed into something or been crashed into because she didn't have the lights on and Lily had been hurt?

She was responsible for Lily now. She had to keep them both safe.

"I have to figure out how to turn on the lights, Lily," she said. Her voice shook, but not too much. She had to be calm for her little sister. "And how the windows work."

She felt Lily's head nod.

She put Lily in the front seat for the moment and got in beside her. The parking lot lights were bright enough for her to explore the area around the driver's seat. She found the stick that controlled the lights, though nothing happened when she moved it. But that was probably because the car wasn't running. And she found a window control pad like Ama's, but in a different place.

"Okay," she told Lily. "I'm going to try this again." She got out of the car and motioned to Lily. "Let's put you in the back where you'll be safer."

Lily shook her head. When she looked at Rose, her eyes caught the light. "Illy. Ose."

"Come on, Lily. You're too little to sit in the front seat."

Lily's brows drew together.

"Okay, okay." Lily couldn't throw a fit now. Rose got the pillow out of the backseat and bundled it around Lily, then fastened the seat belt over the pillow. "Will you stay like that? Even if it isn't really comfortable?"

Lily nodded.

"Okay. But you have to."

Lily nodded again. "Bobble."

Rose found the bottle and gave it to her sister; then she got in, fastened her own seat belt, and started the car. She made the windows go up and down, she made the lights go on and off, bright and dim. Was there anything else she should check?

She hadn't seen any other cars the whole time they'd been in the parking lot. It was so late. It should be easier to drive now.

Gas. She should have thought of that in the apartment parking lot. What if they needed gas? She didn't have money.

She stared at the glowing circle with the picture of the gas pump. It wasn't like Ama's car, but she understood the meaning. The tank was almost empty.

Rose turned off the key. Lily looked at her.

"We're about out of gas," she told Lily. "So we need to make a plan about where to go. We can't just drive around."

Lily kept looking at her with such trust and love. Rose pressed her hands to her head. This was so hard.

"I guess we could just live in the car," she finally said. "We wouldn't need gas for that."

The car was cozy with all their stuff in it, and they could lock the doors and be safe. But the car didn't have a bathroom, and it didn't have water. And Rose was thirsty. Why hadn't she packed water? But what would she have put it in? The cheerful, beat-up red thermos Ama carried on the farm popped into Rose's head. She shoved the memory away.

If they lived right here in this parking lot, they could use the restrooms inside the convenience store. And there would be a water fountain. But somebody might notice a smashed-up car always in the small lot and two kids hanging out in the restroom and not buying anything.

They would blend in better at the mall. Plus, it would be a nicer place to sell her paper art. Plus, there was a fountain where people threw in coins for good luck. The people didn't need the money or they wouldn't have thrown it away. So why couldn't Rose and Lily have it?

"The mall is a better idea," she told Lily.

But Lily, her bottle tucked in between the pillow and the seat belt, had gone back to sleep. And Rose was exhausted too. There was no hurry to get to the mall. She leaned back and shut her eyes for just a minute.

A siren woke her. She jerked her head up and reached for Lily, who was right there beside her and had opened her eyes. The car with the siren came very close, very loud. It whizzed past and the siren sound gradually died away.

Rose rubbed her eyes. The clock on the dashboard always said 12:00, and she had no idea what time it really was. Sometime in the middle of the night or very early morning. There probably wouldn't be many other cars around, so it was a good time to go to the mall.

Lily looked at Rose with trust; then she patted her bottle and babbled something to it.

Rose said, "Okay, Lily, I'm going to start the car." She didn't want to drive again, but she had to. She arranged her book bag, sat up very straight, and turned the key. As the car came to life, she gripped the wheel.

They seemed to be the only car in town. Driving was a lot easier with the lights on.

At a red light, Rose asked Lily if she had ever been to the mall.

When Lily's burst of babbling ran down, Rose said, "They have hot pretzels. And cheese." Though Ama said the cheese had never been acquainted with a cow or any other animal. "When we get money"—when Rose got her art business going—"I will buy you a hot pretzel with cheese."

Lily looked at Rose and clapped, which made Rose laugh. Lily didn't really understand her.

"And there's a cosmetics counter that smells like a whole herd of Aunt Carols."

Lily clapped again.

"Maddy likes to go there, but I think it's kind of boring."

And deep down, Rose didn't really want to live in a place that smelled like hot pretzels and fake cheese and perfume. Everything they touched there would have been touched by who knew how many people's hands and feet and bottoms. Rose didn't really want to live in town.

And then she knew where she was taking Lily, at least for now.

At the next street, she turned right and went around the block. Then she turned left.

As she drove past the courthouse, which had a jail in the basement—maybe where Iris was locked up this very minute—she passed a sheriff sitting in his parked car. Her heart nearly leapt out of her chest, but he didn't look up.

By the time her heart settled down, they were through town and on the highway. The highway was straight and empty, and the lines on either side were bright, so she knew just where to drive. She speeded up a little.

Rose took her eyes off the road for a second and glanced at her sister—who she could see much more clearly because dawn was coming. It was morning. She had never stayed up all night before, though once or twice she and Maddy had tried. Just seeing the pinking sky made her feel like a winner.

·· fifteen ··

ORE cars came onto the road as the sky brightened. But they were all going the other way, toward town, so driving was pretty easy. Rose passed the familiar places. The A-frame building that used to sell carpet but was now a church with a big flashing sign about Jesus. The field where everybody came for Fourth of July fireworks. The fancy house with a white board fence where horses lived.

She looked at the gas gauge once or twice, then quit looking. Either they had enough or they didn't. She knew better than to turn off the highway onto Swan Drive. That route would take them too close to the farmhouse. If Ama happened to be outside, she might see them. So Rose went on to Dove Lane and turned left.

This road was much trickier than the one she drove on the day she followed Ama in the truck. It was very narrow and hilly and curvy. If they met another vehicle, Rose would have to scoot over almost into the ditch. The banks were overgrown with pampas grass and wild honeysuckle and the sky was blooming into pink and orange and gold.

Lily was looking around, her eyes big. Rose opened their windows and let the morning air pour in. The honeysuckle smelled so sweet Lily began to babble—a long, long babble that sounded almost like a song. It reminded Rose of the way birds sing in the morning. Rose felt the same way. When daylight came in the country and the sky unrolled in many colors, how could a bird or a person not sing or babble?

"Lily, have you ever seen anything like it? And wait until we get to the dollhouse! Ama's favorite flowers grow by the toolshed. You can't see them now, but you can in August. They're lilies, just like you."

Lily looked at Rose and crowed something in total delight.

"And you were certainly a surprise!" Rose said, and laughed. She hadn't laughed in a long time. "I love you, Lily," she said. "I just love you to pieces."

At the dollhouse, Rose drove through the tall grass behind the barn where Iris's car couldn't be spotted from the road. She turned off the motor.

Lily escaped from the pillow-and-seat-belt rigging Rose had fastened her into. She stood on the seat and leaned out the window. Her full diaper was about to fall off. She was barefooted.

"Oh, Lily. I forgot your shoes."

Lily looked at her feet, then turned to look at Rose. "Soos," she said.

Rose shook her head. "I messed up. I didn't pack them."

Lily's face darkened. "Soos!"

"I had so much to think about, and we were in a hurry. And I stayed up all night. And I carried you out while you were asleep so you didn't have shoes on." Those were good excuses. She couldn't think of everything.

Lily's face grew darker.

"Please don't throw a fit, Lily."

But it was like saying to the thunder *Please don't chase the lightning.*

"Soos, soos, soos!" Lily screamed, trying to stomp her feet. But she got tangled up in the pillow and fell, arching backward.

Lily's head felt like a bowling ball when it hit Rose's nose.

It really hurt, but she also felt numb. And she felt a strange pressure and then the warm wetness of blood surging out. It ran over her mouth and down her chin. She tasted it and saw it in Lily's hair.

She turned loose of Lily, who flung herself into the pillow and kicked, her feet pummeling Rose's legs. When blood dripped onto Lily's foot, Lily lay suddenly still. But the barn crows had begun to scream. Several crows together were called a murder of crows, and it did sound like someone was being murdered.

Lily's dark eyes searched for the raucous birds. Not understanding, she turned her gaze to Rose.

"Ose?" Her voice had terror in it.

Then a crow, its wings wide and its beak open, thumped

down on the hood of the car and stared through the window at them, first with one eye and then the other. It continued to caw and scream, as did all its friends. Two more landed on the car.

Lily zipped into Rose's arms like a mouse into its hole. Rose's nose was still gushing blood and the blood was getting all over Lily. In terror, Lily tried to wipe it off, all the while pointing at the crows and screaming.

"Shhh, Lily," Rose said, tasting the saltiness of the blood. "Shhh. They're just big birds." She didn't know what else to do so she began to recite the old saying about them. "One for sorrow, two for mirth. Three for a wedding, four for a birth. Five for silver, six for gold. Seven for a secret about to be told."

The crows were quieting down, though a couple on the barn roof were still carrying on like the world was ending.

Rose managed to get her T-shirt off while still cradling Lily. She pressed the shirt to her nostrils to quell the bleeding.

Gradually, while Lily stayed in Rose's arms as still as a stone, even the birds on the barn roof went quiet.

The country silence Rose loved so much began to return. The dew on the barn's tin roof dripped. Small birds went about their business.

And then she heard a familiar diesel rumble.

·· sixteen ··

 *A*S the sound grew closer, Rose sat up, keeping her T-shirt pressed to her nose. What was Ama doing here?

The sound of the engine quit and Rose heard the truck door open. The next thing she knew, Myrtle was flying through the passenger window of Iris's car and bouncing and spinning with excitement. Lily squirmed even closer as Myrtle attacked with love.

Rose had forgotten how Myrtle smelled. She smelled like clover.

Then, as quickly as Myrtle had leapt in the window, she leapt out and made the single yip that said all was well.

Then Rose's door was opened and she almost tumbled out, but Ama caught her.

"Rose!" Ama cried, alarm in her voice. "You're hurt! Oh, my girl. You're bleeding. You're both bleeding! What happened? Where's Iris?"

"In jail! A man came and got her last night! She stole something!" Rose knew she was yelling, but so many feelings were churning around inside they had to come out in yells.

Ama looked so shocked it scared Rose. White-faced, Ama stared at them. "Are you both hurt? What happened?"

Rose's nose was bleeding again and she pressed it with her T-shirt, which muffled her voice. "Lily threw a fit because I forgot her shoes and she accidentally bashed my nose with her head. That's what's bleeding. My nose. Lily isn't bleeding, she just has my blood on her."

Ama still looked terrified.

"We're okay," Rose said. She was holding Lily, which was hard, so she gently put her down. But Lily twined around Rose like honeysuckle.

"Let's get you onto the porch," Ama said. "And see about your nose."

Ama put her arm around Rose and helped her toward the house. Rose felt as if all her bones had been removed, and she just wanted to be in Ama's pocket. She wanted Ama to take care of her.

Lily stayed wrapped around Rose's leg, saying, "Owie, owie," with every step.

Rose remembered. "We have to carry Lily because she's barefooted."

Ama turned loose of Rose and bent to pick up Lily, but Lily shrank back.

"It's all right, Lily," Rose said. With her frightened dark eyes and blood everywhere, Lily looked like a wild thing. "This is Ama."

Ama scooped Lily into her arms. Lily allowed it but kept her eyes on Rose.

"Let's sit in the swing," Ama said when they got to the porch.

Myrtle lay at their feet, and Ama kept Lily on her lap as they sat down. Lily really smelled a lot like pee and she had blood all over her. Rose wished she could have been clean and sweet-smelling and dressed in something cute.

Ama took the bloody T-shirt out of Rose's hands. "Lean your head forward," she said, "so you don't swallow blood."

She'd been swallowing blood? She felt light-headed, like she might be sick.

"Rose," Ama said, patting her leg, "pinch your nose together like this." Ama demonstrated. "Lean forward and do that."

Rose did and gradually the drips of blood slowed and she began to feel better.

"Just keep pinching," Ama said.

It felt so good to be home. Lily was looking at Myrtle with interest. She seemed to have forgotten she was sitting on a stranger's lap.

"How much longer?" Rose asked.

"Just a few minutes," Ama said, rocking the swing gently. "Then we'll see if it's stopped."

Myrtle got up and kissed Lily's bare foot. Lily yanked it away and looked at Ama.

"She likes you," Ama said. "Her name is Myrtle."

Myrtle's ears pricked.

"Myrtle," Ama said again.

Lily touched her chest. "Illy," she told Myrtle. "Ose," she said, touching Rose.

Rose felt such a welling of hope that she overflowed with tears. Didn't Ama see that they had to keep Lily?

Shortly, Ama told Rose to stop pinching and see what happened.

When Rose took her fingers away, her nose felt weird, as if the blood might start flowing again.

"So far, so good," Ama said. "We'll just sit here awhile and make sure it's stopped."

Lily slid off Ama's lap and sat down beside Myrtle. Myrtle sniffed her diaper. Rose didn't mean to laugh, but she did.

"I put her in the car while she was asleep. I don't think she has pajamas. And then I forgot her *s-h-o-e-s*."

"You've had a lot to think about the last couple of days," Ama said. "A lot of responsibility."

"How did you know we were here?" Rose asked.

"Myrtle. She must have caught your scent or heard your voice. In any case, she started going crazy. I had no idea what was wrong. Then I heard the commotion with the crows and came to find out what was going on. Since Myrtle was acting happy instead of aggressive, I had a feeling it might have something to do with you. I was just getting ready to come and get you at Iris's apartment. If Iris was taken away, does that mean you were alone last night?"

Rose nodded.

Ama hugged her. "And I guess you drove all the way out here."

Rose nodded. And it had been so much harder than she thought it would be.

"That was Homeric." Ama kissed her head. "It was also very dangerous."

"I know." Rose was lucky a bloody nose was the worst thing that had happened.

"You're a very brave girl."

Rose felt fluffed up. Ama could always make her feel that way.

"I saw a lot of stuff in the backseat," Ama said. "What is all that?"

Rose told her.

"Were you going on the run?"

"We were maybe going to live at the mall, but I decided I didn't want Lily to live in town."

Ama didn't say anything for a long time. Then she said, "Well, I'm really glad you came here. It's where you belong."

Did Ama mean Lily too?

Lily was exploring Myrtle the same way she explored the mouse book—forward and backward—finding all four of Myrtle's paws, touching them and looking at them, now and then saying things to Myrtle in her babble that Myrtle seemed to understand perfectly. Lily looked under Myrtle's tail, which Myrtle allowed. Myrtle showed Lily her speckled belly and her teeth. She even let Lily look at her gums.

"Rose, I'm sorry I said those terrible things. I'm sorry I—"

Rose shook her head, tears flooding her eyes. She needed time to catch up with herself. She held up her hand for Ama to stop talking.

"Okay," Ama said.

And they sat in silence.

Finally, Ama said, "Let's go home and get you cleaned up."

Rose nodded.

seventeen

*T*HEY stacked all their stuff in the laundry room. Myrtle kept looking at the box with the ham in it. Rose didn't have to worry about enough food for her and Lily now, so she opened the box and fed Myrtle a piece of ham.

"Thanks for finding us," she whispered.

While the bathtub filled, she took off Lily's diaper and lifted her into the tub. They didn't have bubble bath or tub toys. Then she remembered. Her old bathtub toys were in a mesh bag under the sink.

She dumped the toys into the water and then took off her own bloody clothes and got in.

She lay back until only her face was sticking out, then held her nose and slid all the way under. She listened to Lily's splashing noises. It felt so good to not be running or lying or hiding or planning or driving. To be home and tucked under Ama's wing again. Had she really been so hurt and angry she'd run away? But if she hadn't run away, she might not have found Lily. She might never have had the chance to get to know her mother a little.

When Rose surfaced for air, Ama was in the room gathering up bloody clothes. Rose heard the washer filling.

"Lily is playing with your old tub toys," Ama remarked.

Rose nodded. "Were they anyone else's before they were mine?"

Ama sat on the edge of the tub and looked at each one. "Only this one," she said, picking up the turtle toy. "It was mine. I remember Annie winding it up for me when I was little. Or maybe I only think I remember that. Maybe I actually recall Annie telling me about it."

Ama twisted the tail to wind it up, and then she put it in the water and turned it loose. The big turtle with the baby on her back kicked her legs as she swam through the water until she bumped into Lily's belly.

Lily snatched the toy out of the water. "Ose!" she said. "Illy!"

Rose laughed. "If you say so."

Ama smiled. "And history repeats itself," she said. "How do bacon and eggs sound? And I picked a few strawberries yesterday."

Fresh eggs and nice crispy bacon sounded heavenly. "I'll bet Lily has never had a strawberry right out of the garden," Rose said.

After Ama went to the kitchen, Rose cleaned Lily's body with a washcloth and shampooed her hair. Rose was so glad to be home, but Ama had said they couldn't keep Lily. And Rose understood now how much trouble babies were. But Rose had to keep Lily. She'd found her and she had to take care of her.

When Rose and Lily were dressed and sitting side by side on the bench around the kitchen table, Rose tilted her empty plate to the light. She could see her reflection. Squeaky-clean dishes were amazing. She caught Ama looking at her and put the plate down. But she noticed her glistening fork and spoon in a new way too.

Ama had also set a fork and spoon for Lily, who sat very close to Rose. Rose hoped Ama didn't mind that Lily ate with her fingers.

Lily gazed around the kitchen, her eyes going to the windows. Tree branches moved in the wind, showing patches of bright blue sky. Her brows furrowed, she looked up at the high ceiling, where a fan turned slowly. When the clock began the chimes her eyes widened, and as it bonged nine o'clock she looked at Rose with worry in her eyes.

"It's okay," Rose said.

Lily was still hanging on to the bathtub turtle. "Illy. Ose," Lily said, showing it to Rose again.

"I made some phone calls while you were in the tub," Ama said.

Rose felt like her heart had been dropped in ice water. She stared at Ama. Was this about Lily? Had Ama called someone to come and get Lily?

"I was trying to find out exactly what happened to Iris."

Rose shut her eyes for a second. "Did you find out?"

"The man who came to the apartment and took her away was a federal marshal." Ama sounded tired, and she looked sad. "When Iris lived in Kentucky, she stole mail from a neighboring family's mailbox and applied for credit cards in their name. And then a couple of years ago she used the credit cards to buy things." Ama's eyes went to Lily.

"Why are you looking at Lily? Did she buy *Lily*?" Rose would die if she had to give Lily back.

Ama looked startled. "No! Why would you think that?"

"She doesn't look like us. Not even a little bit."

Ama shook her head. "She doesn't look like the Lovells. But those wide-set dark eyes of hers are just like the Smiths." Ama brushed Lily's curls off her forehead. "And see this V shape of her hairline? That's called a widow's peak. Just like her grandfather's."

Rose didn't like her grandfather, but she was giddy to know that he had passed on some things to Lily. "Anything else?" she asked.

"It's hard to tell with a toddler," Ama said. "But I'm pretty sure Lily is going to have his hands and feet."

Rose snatched up both of Lily's hands and kissed them. And then she kissed her feet.

Lily pushed Rose away.

"The timing of Iris's crime," Ama said, "makes me wonder if Iris stole to buy things she needed for a new baby."

Rose could tell from Ama's eyes that Ama wanted to believe this, so she nodded. But all Lily had in the apartment was a dirty, bare mattress and a few ratty clothes.

Ama went on explaining what she'd found out. "Iris will appear before a federal judge Monday and most likely be charged with a felony. And a trial date will be set. That will probably be in a few months. On Monday, the judge will decide whether Iris can be released on bail or if she needs to stay locked up until the trial."

With every word, Ama looked sadder, but she scooped bacon and eggs onto their plates.

Rose didn't understand everything Ama had said, and she didn't want to make Ama talk about Iris any more than she had to. Iris might be staying in jail for a long time. Or she might not. Rose hated the uncertainty. Until recently, everything in her life had been as predictable as the sunrise.

Ama set a bowl of fresh strawberries on the table. A few of the strawberries still had their leaves and stems, so it was almost like eating them in the strawberry patch. Rose would take Lily to the strawberry patch later. And the pea patch.

Ama ate with them. Lily knelt on the bench and used her fingers, though she watched Rose and Ama use their glistening forks. Rose pulled the green cap off a small strawberry and ate the red part. Lily watched. Then Rose pulled the green cap off another and offered the berry to Lily. Lily put it in her mouth. As she chewed, her eyes came to Rose's in surprise.

"Yum!" Rose said, eating another one.

"Um!" Lily said. Then she spat it out and looked at the drooly red mess.

"Yuck!" Rose said.

"Uck!" Lily agreed, trying to hand it to Rose.

Rose got a piece of paper towel and took the messy berry and wiped Lily's fingers.

The food was making Rose feel heavy and tired. And her nose was hurting and her eye was swelling. She could stretch out on the bench and fall sleep. But she had to take care of Lily.

"The court didn't know Iris had a second child," Ama said. "But now they do."

"You told them!" Rose gasped.

"Iris told them. She was worried about the two of you alone in the apartment."

Rose didn't understand grown-ups. Iris did bad, stupid stuff and she was a terrible mother. Still, she was worried about them being on their own.

Ama touched Rose's shoulder. "You look done in. And we need to get ice on that eye. Why don't I make an ice pack and you lie down on your bed for a while."

It sounded so good Rose almost closed her eyes thinking about it.

But she forced them wide open. "Okay. But I want Lily to lie down with me."

\#

Rose led Lily upstairs. They went slowly because Lily wanted to stop and look between all the posts to make sure Myrtle was still in the foyer. Rose wanted to show Lily the wardrobe where the dolls were, but she was too tired.

"Come on, Lily," she said, tugging her sister's hand.

But Lily wanted to look in every room as they went down the hall.

"Let's go see *my* room, Lily," Rose said, trying to sound enthusiastic.

Rose felt as if she'd been gone for a hundred years. Her big bed with its silently singing birds called to her.

When Rose lifted Lily into it, Lily looked startled. Rose fluffed a pillow for Lily, then fluffed one for herself. She kicked off her shoes. They'd have to go to town tomorrow and buy Lily shoes—also clothes that hadn't been worn by someone else. Rose had forty-one dollars in the trunk from origami and dog sitting.

Rose stretched out. It felt so good to be in her own bed, with her own pillow. She groaned. "Oh, Lily, let's have a long nap."

Lily lay on her side, watching Rose. She cradled the bath-tub toy.

Rose shut her eyes and pressed the ice pack to her face. Her last thought was about Peanutbutter. She needed to go see her calf.

#

When Rose woke up, the comfort of her bed tangled her muscles and tried to pull her under. She almost went back to sleep.

But she opened her eyes. The room was dim with late-day light.

Where was Lily?

Rose sat up and looked around the room. Something smelled funny.

She stared. What had happened to the wall below her shadow boxes? Why were there thick black marks all over the wallpaper? And what was that smell?

She stepped on the lid of her permanent marker. The tip stuck out from under the bed. And her bedspread had black streaks down the sides.

Anger pounded in her ears. How could Lily do such a thing? The wallpaper was ruined. The bedspread was ruined. Now, Rose saw, Lily had messed with all her art supplies.

She heard Ama's voice.

Across the hall, at the secret listening post, with shaking hands, Rose pulled away the piece of baseboard.

"Rose wore these when she was about your size. She liked the sound they made when she pulled the Velcro strap, so she was always taking them off and I was always putting them back on." Rose heard a ripping noise. "Let's see how they fit you."

"Soos!" Lily crowed.

Feelings Rose didn't understand churned so hard she

thought she might throw up. She felt angry and happy and grateful and jealous. And furious.

She crossed the hall and snatched up the turtle toy Lily had left on the bed and snapped the little turtle off the big turtle's back. She dropped the pieces on the bed. Then she threw herself down and buried her face in her pillow. She wanted Lily to be in time-out forever, yet she wanted to take care of her sister— teach her how to eat with a spoon and talk and pick strawberries.

When she went downstairs, she told Ama what Lily had done, but Ama already knew. Lily had come down with marker all over herself.

"Toddlers are curious, so they get into stuff. They try everything to see how it works or how it tastes. At least she didn't put the marker in her mouth. That would have made her sick." She gave Rose a long look. "Toddlers have to be watched every second. They keep a person busy."

"But my room is ruined," Rose said.

"Not your whole room. Your bedspread needs to be updated anyway. And we can do something about the east wall. Paint it?" she suggested.

Rose liked to paint. And Lily looked awfully cute and proud in her shiny new shoes.

# #

Later in the day, the three of them walked to the barn to take care of Peanutbutter. Ama carried Lily because, as Ama said, she wanted to get there before morning.

206

Myrtle swung out in circles to sniff. When she swung back to them, she always paid special attention to Lily. Lily liked that, but every time a cow bawled, she shrank closer to Ama.

At the barn, Ama stayed outside with Lily while Rose went into the shop and made Peanutbutter's bottle.

In her pen, Peanutbutter danced with excitement.

"I told you Rose would be back," Ama said.

Peanutbutter bumped the bottle, nearly knocking it out of Rose's hands, then began to suck.

"I missed you," Rose said. "You've grown." Rose had been gone only three days, but Peanutbutter really did look bigger. "You're still adorable."

"God makes all nature's babies adorable so we can't help but love them and care for them," Ama said.

Rose couldn't see Ama's face in the shadows, but the snapshot of Iris with her big stomach and Rose all folded up inside flitted through her mind. When she was born, her mother hadn't been able to love her and care for her. That was just the way it was. Thank goodness Ama had stepped up.

The dew-filled air was fresh and cool. Ama walked around with Lily talking to her while Rose finished her nightly routine. When she opened the record book, she saw that Ama had made entries while Rose was gone. Ama had led Peanutbutter around the barnyard every evening, keeping her in practice.

"Thank you for taking care of Peanutbutter while I was gone," Rose said.

"You're welcome."

Ama put her arm around Rose's shoulders as they walked to the house, Ama again carrying Lily. Rose leaned against Ama's side. Lily's foot, wearing Rose's baby shoe, pressed against Rose's ribs. It kind of hurt, and it felt really good. "Bobble," Lily said softly without much interest.

She startled when a whippoorwill sang from the fencerow. Rose loved the shy birds you never saw because of their camouflage, and Lily would come to love them too.

#

The little shoes weren't the only things Ama had kept. In a basket Rose had never seen, they found soft black-and-yellow-striped pajamas.

"Do you remember them?" Ama asked.

Rose shook her head. But she put them on Lily, who smelled of toothpaste. "You look like a cute little bumblebee," she told her sister.

"I know you couldn't possibly remember this," Ama said, holding up a rose-colored sacklike thing with long sleeves and tiny mittens at the end and a little hood with a creamy silk lining.

Rose laughed. "No!"

"That was for your first winter," Ama said. "How about this?" She shook out a ballerina's sparkly silver-and-white tutu with a black velvet leotard.

"Yes!" Rose said—though she didn't really remember

wearing it, only seeing pictures of herself on Halloween when she was three or four.

Ama held up a little hoodie. "You were wearing this the first time you really noticed the wind. I carried you outside and the wind blew back the hood. You bounced with excitement and made a noise as if you were naming the wind. It sounded like *Heeeee*. I thought of that as your first word."

Ama kept unfolding clothes and telling Rose stories about her babyhood, while Lily and Myrtle played.

"Why have you never told me these stories before?" Rose asked. "I didn't even know you kept these clothes."

"Since you didn't ask, I thought maybe you didn't want to know."

"I thought you didn't want to talk about it," Rose said. "Because you never did. I like to know. Even the hard parts. Iris told me a lot of stuff."

A look of uncertainty flickered on Ama's face.

"She told me you didn't know I was coming. You didn't even know I existed."

"Oh, Rose, I'm so sorry I spoke those terrible words the other night."

Rose tried not to cry when she said, "They broke my heart. But I understand better now." Her throat aching with held-back tears, she said, "I know you love me."

"Can you forgive me?" Ama asked.

Rose nodded. She couldn't find her voice for her tears.

Ama wiped Rose's tears with her fingers, though she was crying too. "Don't cry," she said.

"Then don't *you* cry," Rose said, wiping Ama's tears.

Ama rewrapped the clothing that didn't fit Lily and put it away. When the basket was back in the closet, she sat down by Rose on the bed. "I didn't know you existed, and I wasn't expecting you. And it took me a while to adjust. But in no time, I felt you bringing happiness back into my life. My mom's days were coming to an end, and it was such a comfort to hold the warm bundle of you against my chest. Babies are like holding hope. That's what you became to me. Hope."

Rose fell into her arms and Ama folded her close, kissing her hair.

#

Later, when Lily was sprawled in the middle of Rose's bed deeply asleep, Rose got up and turned on her desk lamp. She took the broken turtle out of the drawer where she'd hidden it from Lily and used superglue to reattach the little turtle to the big one. Hopefully, Lily would never find out what Rose had done.

·· eighteen ··

AMA said the lady who visited on Friday just wanted information, but Rose was terrified she planned to take Lily away. She carried a briefcase and looked quickly and carefully at absolutely everything. Rose wanted to keep Lily in her room, but Ama said the lady had to see Lily and make sure she was okay.

Rose felt a huge wave of relief when the woman began by saying both Iris and the court had approved Lily's staying with Ama for now.

"And me," Rose said. "I'm her sister, and I take care of her. I'm responsible."

She slept with Lily. She bathed and dressed her, brushed her teeth, changed her diapers, took her everywhere. Showed her everything.

Rose had shown her sister all the rooms, the wardrobe full of dolls, the mailbox, the porch swing, the rope swing. The big golden hay bales, the garden, the barn, the cows, the fall calves that were almost heifers, the spring calves that were about the size of Peanutbutter. The truck, both tractors, the grain drill, the corn picker, the hay baler, the silage cutter, the riding mower, the garden tiller. The creek, the ponds, lots of birds and butterflies, toads and frogs, fish, rabbits, squirrels, a fox, and the big bull snake that lived in the barn.

Lily had shown Rose things too. A white clover blossom, without its stem. An anthill. A twig caught in the grass. A tiny speckled pebble. A ladybug.

Sometimes Lily went so slowly Rose wanted to snatch her up and carry her, but Ama said they should encourage Lily to be independent. Rose had given Lily one of her old baby dolls, which Lily didn't like. Ama said perhaps Lily was jealous of it.

The last couple of days, Lily had learned about a million words—*calf, clock, pj's, Ama, please, turtle, muffin, stairs, bed, sister, drink,* and more. When the lady with the briefcase asked Lily her name, Lily told her. She also introduced Rose, Ama, and Myrtle. Lily was like a beautiful clear bottomless glass that they could just keep pouring things into.

Ama kept telling Rose not to get attached. She kept reminding Rose that Lily didn't belong to them. *But she could,* Rose wanted to say, because Iris didn't want her. Rose's hope was that the longer Lily stayed, the more likely Ama was to love her.

"Of course," the lady with the briefcase explained, "Lily belongs to Iris. But until Iris's future is known, and as long as she's incarcerated, are you willing to have temporary custody?"

"Yes," Rose said.

"For now," Ama said. "We'll see what happens on Monday."

Before she left, the lady gave Ama a card with the jail's visiting hours. She said they were all three on the approved visitors' list. Ama put the card in her pocket without reading it.

#

That afternoon, Rose led Lily upstairs and gave her paper and crayons. Ama and Myrtle were busy bringing the spring calves and their mamas up to the barn. Tomorrow the vet would come and vaccinate the calves and castrate the little bulls. Rose took the crayons away when Lily put them in her mouth. She gave Lily books to look at, but Lily wanted Rose to read them to her, or she wanted to read them to Rose.

"Book, Ose!" Lily said, taking Rose's face in her hands to claim Rose's attention.

Rose wanted to be at her desk. She had an idea for making a fish mobile to hang in front of the potty chair Ama had installed in the bathroom. Ama had brought it down from the attic, where it had been since Rose was little. Lily didn't like to sit on it. Rose was going to fold a whole school of fish out of waxed paper and build a mobile that would make sitting on the potty chair more interesting for her sister.

Or she might do some other kind of paper art. Something she hadn't thought of yet. Something that would just come to her the way ideas did. But it was hard to think or have ideas when Lily kept taking Rose's face in her hands and saying, "Ose!"

#

That night, after she'd read Lily to sleepiness, then rubbed her back to finish the job, Rose went downstairs to brush Ama's hair. The lamplight and the smell of angelica drifting through the window made Rose want to curl up on Ama's bed. But she needed to sleep with Lily in case she woke up.

"Before you brush my hair," Ama said, "let me trim your bangs. They're falling in your eyes."

Ama had said that very same thing last Sunday—only a few days ago. But since last Sunday, Rose's heart had broken and mended, she'd discovered her sister, she'd gotten to know her mother a little.

Rose and Ama stood face to face, Ama in her striped pajamas, Rose in her blue nightie. Ama's breath brushed Rose as Ama held Rose's bangs between her fingers.

"Shut your eyes," she said.

The familiar *scritch* of the scissors cutting her hair lasted only a couple of minutes. Rose wished it had lasted longer.

Ama blew lightly on Rose's face to clear away tiny hairs and said, "There, now you can see the world again. And the world can see you."

Rose stood behind Ama and brushed her hair, forgetting to count—trying to build up courage. Finally, she just blurted out, "Iris told me you were really Harriet Jane's daughter. Is that true?"

Ama waited a few seconds before she said, "Yes." After a

while, she added, "Strange. It's affected my life so much, but I never talk about it."

"So we're alike," Rose said. "We both had mothers that didn't keep us." If she was going to be like somebody, she was glad it was Ama.

"Except you've always known you were my granddaughter, and that you had a mother out there somewhere. I didn't know until I was eighteen and Harriet Jane came home from Italy after my dad died that I wasn't who I thought I was."

Ama told her about finding out on a hot August day in the cemetery.

"Annie didn't know either. Mom and Harriet Jane told us at the same time that we weren't sisters like we'd always thought. They felt we needed to know."

"So is it still a secret?" Rose asked. "And that's why we did the family tree wrong?"

"It doesn't need to be a secret anymore. Nobody cares. We did the family tree that way because I grew up and lived my life as Clara and Ralph Hoffmann's daughter, with four older sisters. That's who I am."

"Were you upset when they told you?" Rose asked.

"It was upsetting to hear that nothing I'd known and loved my whole life was true or real. The dad I adored, who taught me to love farming, was so unbending that he wouldn't forgive Harriet Jane even a little bit for her choices. He banished her.

He did let Mom go out and stay with her the last five months of her pregnancy, and see her through my birth, then bring me home as his daughter. Everybody just loved me to pieces as I was growing up, but how harsh he was to Harriet Jane. Nobody deserves to be shut out of the family."

Rose wondered if Ama was thinking of Lily, or even Iris, when she said nobody deserved to be shut out of the family.

#

Ama reached up and took Rose's hand and stopped the brushing. She pulled Rose around to sit on the floor between her knees and began to brush Rose's hair.

"Could we change the family tree?" Rose asked. "Move you, Iris, and me to where we belong? And add Lily."

"We can change it on paper," Ama said after a while. "But where a person fits in her family isn't that black-and-white."

"Why is our last name Lovell?" Rose asked. "Shouldn't it be Smith?"

"Long story," Ama said.

"Tell me."

"When my mother—who was really my grandmother—was a girl . . ."

"Clara," Rose said.

"Yes, Clara. When she was about your age, everybody who lived along the road for a couple of miles was a Lovell. Your great-great-great-grandfather Lovell had four sons, and those men all farmed and raised their families out here. My mom

216

used to tell me stories about them. Her aunts and uncles and cousins. She told me who had horses. Who had puppies. She told me about the Great Depression. About the first tractor. About well water and outhouses. About the organ in the parlor of her grandparents' house." Ama sighed. "They were all Lovells. Then Mom—Clara—married a Hoffmann, and her four daughters were Hoffmanns. But when Harriet Jane ran off and bad blood developed between her and her dad, Harriet Jane changed her name. Not only her first name, but her last name."

"Lotus Lovell," Rose said.

"Yes. And she named me Tulip Lovell. That's what my birth certificate says, though I had no idea until I found out I was Harriet Jane's daughter. And when I married Larry, I took his name, Smith, but went back to Lovell after the divorce. And when I adopted you, I gave you the Lovell name."

"I would rather be a Lovell than a Hoffmann or a Smith," Rose said. "For one thing, it begins with *love*."

Ama patted her shoulder. "People around here probably thought it was odd. It probably made some suspect what others had already figured out—that I was Harriet Jane's child. But nobody cared anymore. All this land was once owned by Lovells. It supported five families for years. People always called the farm the Lovell place."

They were quiet for a while as Ama brushed. "Just think of the family tree as a little wrinkled," Ama finally said. "I imagine most family trees are."

Rose nodded. "You want to hear a lame riddle?" she asked.

"Sure."

"Pete and Repeat were sitting on a fence. Pete fell off. Who was left?"

Ama groaned. "Oh, that is lame. You won't believe how far back in our family that silly riddle goes. Where did you hear it?"

"From Iris."

Ama was quiet.

Rose actually liked the riddle. At first, she'd agreed with her mother that the riddle described Iris, making the same mistakes repeatedly. But the more she learned about her family tree, the more she suspected they had all made mistakes, some of which were repeated by the next generation. Or the next.

"Who in the family tree am I most like?" she asked.

"I'm sure you've noticed you look like your mother," Ama said. "Except she has Annie's freckles and you don't."

Rose nodded. She was gradually getting comfortable with looking a little like her mother.

"And I think you love the farm as much as I do," Ama went on. "And you're brave and bold and creative like Harriet Jane."

Rose smiled, though Ama couldn't see.

"The way you've devoted yourself to Lily and just naturally understood how to take care of her may be Clara's genes coming through."

Ama quit brushing and laid down the brush.

Rose sat there for a while, leaning against Ama.

When they'd made the family tree and Rose had given her oral report, everybody except Ama had been just a name with dates and events and a few stories. Sort of like down the road at the cemetery on Memorial Day. But now she was starting to feel those people as part of her. She looked at her hands, which were like her mother's. They made her feel more complicated. And scared. And strong.

nineteen

THE day before Iris's arraignment in court was rainy. Lily was cranky and threw a fit when Rose tried to get her to sit on the potty chair. She screamed so loud Myrtle went out on the porch. And she kicked the potty chair so hard it fell over.

Rose sat on the edge of the bathtub watching her sister writhe on the floor. "Oh, Lily," she said.

Lily stopped for a second, then screamed louder.

Ama came in and sat beside Rose. Lily's screaming was making Rose's head hurt, but it didn't seem right to go off and leave her. Rose longed for a pajama day—one of those rainy summer days when she didn't have to do anything at all, not even get dressed. The things she might do flickered through her mind, and they involved paper and creativity and quiet. Though today was probably ruined no matter what because of worry about what would happen tomorrow.

Gradually, Lily wound down, and when Ama opened her arms, Lily let Ama cuddle her.

Sometimes Rose didn't like Ama cuddling Lily so much— especially when Lily was being a pill.

"Did I act like that?" Rose asked, certain Ama would say no.

"Yes, you did," Ama said.

"Really?"

"You outgrew it, and so will Lily. And then life will be sweet and calm until teen age. And then it will all start up again."

Rose wasn't going to be stormy in teen age. But how did she know that for sure? She used to know things for sure, but not any longer.

"When Iris hit teen age, your grandfather and I were getting divorced," Ama said. "I should have been a better mother."

Rose wouldn't have believed that a week ago.

"I'm ashamed of the ways I let her down." Ama looked miserable when she said, "And I hid my shame behind anger."

How could Ama have been so different then?

"When Harriet Jane came home and I found out the truth, I didn't know who I was for a while. I think that's why I went off to college and drifted toward things that weren't me. And when I tried to get back where I belonged . . . here . . . I was married to somebody who didn't know me at all. Who couldn't understand my roots. Poor Iris fell into the large, lonely space between us."

Iris looked lonely in the few pictures Rose had seen in the photo albums.

Ama was cradling Lily when she said, "I did not do right by Iris. Maybe that's why she's such a hapless soul."

"Hapless?"

"Unlucky. She couldn't help who her parents were. When she was born." Ama reached out and put her hand on Rose's cheek. "You turned up at the worst of times and the best of times." Ama took a deep breath and let it out. "I do love you, sweet Rose. More than words can say."

Tears came to Rose's eyes and she nodded. "I know," she whispered. Now if Ama would just fold Lily into their lives to stay . . .

The rain, which had let up for a while, began to come down like it was being poured out of a giant bucket. Wind gusted against the window and the lights dimmed but came back on.

Ama sighed. "I'm not going to be able to do anything on the farm today. It will be too wet even if the rain stops." She stared at the wet window. "Let's make cookies. To keep our minds off tomorrow."

#

In the kitchen, they got out cookie sheets. Lily turned a plastic bowl upside down over the tiny flexible dolls from Aunt Carol. It reminded Rose of how she'd felt in Iris's apartment, squeezed together and penned in without air or light.

"Let the dolls out, Lily," Rose said.

Lily ignored her.

Rose didn't want Lily to throw another fit, so she didn't tell her again. And anyway, dolls didn't really have feelings. Even if they did, what was the difference between being under a mixing bowl and being inside an old wardrobe? Either place was dark and stuffy. Rose had hated living in Iris's apartment so much she decided she'd run upstairs later and free the dolls from the wardrobe. She was too old to play with them, but they could live in Great-aunt Phoebe's room—all of them together. Old musty ones, shiny plastic ones, chatty ones, cuddly ones.

"Why do you think my mother is so messy?" she asked Ama.

Ama paused where she was getting out ingredients. "I don't know. I can tell you Annie was a terrible slob. I was always picking up after her, and I was the little sister."

Really? Aunt Annie the doctor?

Ama creamed the butter and sugars with the mixer. While she did that, Rose measured the flour, baking soda, and salt. When the cookie dough was finally ready, they washed Lily's hands and let her help drop dough onto the baking sheets.

"Watch she doesn't put any in her mouth," Ama said. "Raw eggs."

Sure enough, Lily's hand, holding a wad of dough, moved toward her mouth.

"No, no," Rose said. "It will make you sick."

Lily dropped the dough and Myrtle hurried to snarf it up. "No, no!" Lily said. "Sick!" She looked at Rose. "Ose!"

"It's okay," Rose said. "It probably won't make Myrtle sick because she's a dog. But it might, so don't drop any more."

"Otay," Lily said.

Rose beamed. Another word. In the few days they'd been home, Lily had fluffed up, brightened up, cheered up. And she'd gotten heavier and taller, or so it seemed to Rose. Lily was changing as fast as Peanutbutter, who was now walking around the barnyard with Rose without fuss.

Caring for Lily was so much easier with Ama's company, in a big cozy house, eating yummy food.

"Do you think if Iris lived here with us she might be a good mother to Lily?" Rose asked.

A whole merry-go-round of emotions crossed Ama's face. And just posing the question made Rose feel dizzy. She hadn't really meant to ask it.

Ama didn't say anything. She kept dropping dough on the baking sheet. When it was full, she slid it into the oven. Then she asked Rose, "Is that something you want?"

Ama's face was now blank of expression as she looked at Rose, waiting for an answer.

What Rose really wanted was for things to go back the way they were before, when life was perfectly simple and perfectly happy and perfectly predictable. But she had found Lily, and now the way things were before, could never be again.

"If Iris comes to live here, she might decide to leave again and want to take Lily with her," Rose said. And Lily was putting down roots and blossoming like a real flower. "And if she took Lily . . ." Rose looked into Ama's eyes. "I would have to go too." She felt sick saying it. She wasn't even sure she'd be able to do it. But she'd have to try. She couldn't let Lily go back to being all on her own with a mother who didn't pay attention to her.

Iris was like a squirrel—pretty and fun and interesting—but who knew what she might do next? She didn't think far enough ahead to bury a few walnuts.

"Do *you* want Iris to live here?" Rose asked Ama.

Ama was washing Lily's hands when she said, "I don't know. After you got settled in with me, I didn't want her around you. But that was a long time ago."

"That time she came to visit, when I was little, were you angry with me for sitting on her lap?"

"Oh no, Rose. Did you think that?"

Rose nodded. "All these years I thought I'd done something so bad I couldn't even remember it. I asked Iris about the visit and she told me."

Ama touched Rose's cheek. Her hands smelled like soap and cookie dough. "As you've probably noticed, Iris tends to turn up without warning. That morning, I'd taken Myrtle out and I came back inside and you were on her lap and her arms were around you. I thought she'd come to take you. And I went a little crazy. But I never thought you did anything wrong."

Rose felt as if she'd been walking around most of her life with a pebble in her shoe and had just gotten rid of it.

Ama made a cup of coffee and sat down on the bench at the kitchen table. Lily climbed up beside her and onto her lap.

Automatically, Ama's arms went around Lily and she kissed her on the head.

"Assuming Iris won't have to stay in jail until the trial, her living here would really change things," Ama said.

That was what worried Rose.

"It might not work," Ama said.

Rose shook her head in agreement. "Maybe Iris is mainly lonely."

Ama sighed. "I'm sorry for that." She was playing with Lily's dark curls. "Iris is probably not going to give up her friends or her habits," she said.

After what felt like a long time, she added, "But I'd like a chance at a do-over. It won't be perfect. But maybe it won't be a disaster. And even if it fails, the world won't end."

Rose felt the truth of that. Her old, perfect world *had* ended. But a world that wasn't so perfect could live a long time. Just look at the messed-up Lovell family tree. Yet here she was.

·· twenty ··

$\int$CHOOL was starting in a week and Rose had a new hair-style. One Sunday morning, when it was still cool and the smell of the hay Ama had cut the day before hung in the air, Rose and Iris had gone onto the porch. Iris had laid out scissors and clippers she'd borrowed from the salon. She'd fastened a cape around Rose and gone to work. Iris remembered the four things Rose had said in the apartment to describe herself—especially that she wanted to be some kind of artist when she grew up and that she could do anything she set her mind to.

Iris had worked silently for a long time. Haircuts from Ama took two minutes and Rose knew exactly how she would look when Ama was done. The same way she'd looked before. But Rose felt her hair and head being touched in a way that was new. It felt unsettling.

When Iris finally led her into the bathroom, Rose stared at herself in the mirror. She'd been reshaped into a clearer version of herself. She looked taller. The bob emphasized her jawline so she could see the Hoffmann stubbornness. And this new girl, with the long neck and lively gaze, might well grow up to be an artist.

When Maddy got home from England and saw Rose's haircut, she begged Iris to style her hair too. Maddy had seen and done a lot across the pond, as Aunt Carol called the Atlantic Ocean. She'd gotten to know her cousins. She'd seen the Tower of London and Big Ben. She'd gone on a Harry Potter tour and a Buckingham Palace tour. She'd taken a cruise down the Thames. Maddy could hardly believe she'd come back to find Iris in her old room across the hall from Rose.

It was different having Iris in the house. At first, it had been really uncomfortable. Rose wasn't used to sharing, and now she had to share with Iris as well as Lily. And Rose was used to the upstairs belonging only to her. She was used to freedom and privacy.

The first few days, Rose had absolutely hated having Iris there. Rose couldn't settle in at night because Iris was rustling around and her cell phone was always making noises. She left things like apple cores in her room and the smell bothered Rose. Some days Iris didn't get up to go to work. She kept the door shut and came out only to use the bathroom. When Rose saw her in the hall, Iris looked as if the saddest thing in the world had happened and she could never be happy again. But in a day or two, she was back to work and her usual carefree and careless self.

Rose could tell Ama was struggling too. Once, when Iris stayed out all night, Ama was in tears when Rose came downstairs in the morning. And Ama and Iris were stiff with each other. They didn't actually argue, but there was no ease between them. They didn't have any special routines. They didn't know each other's hearts the way Ama and Rose did.

The trial before the judge was next month, and Iris might be going to prison, depending on the outcome. Rose felt guilty and selfish because secretly sometimes she wanted her mother to go to prison and let Rose get back to normal. But normal was gone forever because of Lily. Lily made Rose's heart swell until she could feel love, like a heart-shaped balloon, lifting her higher than she had ever been before.

And Rose was even coming to love Iris a little because they were getting to know each other. She didn't think of Iris as her mother, just as Ama hadn't thought of Harriet Jane as her mother. Rose didn't really have a mother and that was okay because she had Ama, her polestar. But a little love for her hapless mother felt good when it stirred. Iris was generous in styling everybody's hair. She generally meant well. She asked questions and was interested. She told stories about her grandma Clara and the dollhouse. She paid more attention to Lily.

Lily was starting to put words together. She said *I wub you* and *Good dog, Myrtle*. She knew her body parts, although she confused her elbows and her eyebrows. She was ninety-five percent good on her potty training except at night. She had a

youth bed now in Rose's baby bedroom across the hall from
Ama. Sometimes Lily slept there; sometimes she got into bed
with Rose or Ama or Myrtle.

After Lily moved downstairs, Rose painted the ruined wall
the color everybody said would be perfect. Rose. And she got a
new bedspread and pillow shams that looked less babyish.

Even though she didn't think of Iris as her mother, she was.
So Rose had pinned the snapshot of big-bellied Iris on the bulletin board beside the photo of Great-grandma Harriet Jane. And
she had redrawn the family tree, putting all the flower names –
Tulip, Iris, Rose, and Lily – under Lotus, where they belonged.

Pictures of Rose and Peanutbutter had recently been added
to the bulletin board. One of Peanutbutter and Rose looking
scared but ready. A group shot of all the kids with their bottle
calves. And another of Peanutbutter back in her pen with a blue
ribbon on the gate.

Sometimes at night as Rose looked at the stars and the angel in
the cemetery, her mind drifted into the murky *what if.* What if
Iris went to prison? What if Iris didn't go to prison? What if one
day Iris just took Lily and left? What if, someday, something
happened to Ama? What if she, Rose, grew up and really did
become an artist? What if Lily slept in Rose's bed one day?

Rose often had trouble falling asleep. It was like she could
feel herself growing the same way she could hear the popping
sounds of the corn growing during the hot, humid August

nights. On those nights, she went to her desk and folded paper. It might be an animal for Lily or a fanciful star. It might be a box for Ama to keep paper clips in. It might be something she'd never thought of before. She loved the sturdy, forgiving paper that could be folded, unfolded, and refolded until she got it right.

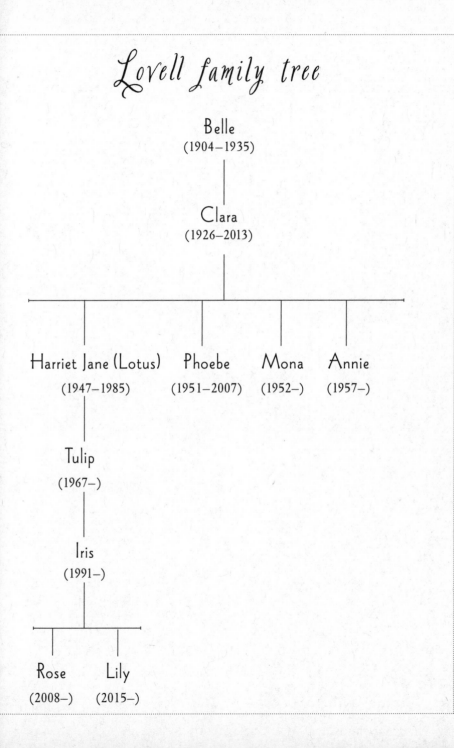

Lovell family tree

Belle
(1904–1935)

Clara
(1926–2013)

Harriet Jane (Lotus)
(1947–1985)

Phoebe
(1951–2007)

Mona
(1952–)

Annie
(1957–)

Tulip
(1967–)

Iris
(1991–)

Rose
(2008–)

Lily
(2015–)